Sins o

Thelonious Legend

This was going to be a special year for the Parker sisters. Eve was going to dominate in the classroom and on the basketball court. Gwen was going to make the starting five and go down in history as the greatest prankster ever. Ana was going to do as little as possible. But without warning, all three sisters gain extraordinary abilities that defy science… powers that come with a cost. Now all they want to do is make it through the school year without drawing any undue attention, while racing to find a cure before the side effects of their new abilities kill them. Eve's temperament, Gwen's fondness for pranks, and Ana's predilection for money, however, are challenges they must overcome to achieve their goals. Because if they can't, they're dead…

"What I wanted most for my daughter was that she be able to soar confidently in her own sky, whatever that may be."

— Helen Claes

For my daughters.

Nothing is beyond your reach.

Geri, my wife, my partner in crime, and my best friend; we got next.

Dedicated to Delores Williams 1948-2014

Mom, you are missed more then you could ever know and I promise to pay forward everything that you invested in me.

Prologue

"He broke free! He's out!"

A pale, bald male of medium build sprinted down a long, dimly lit hallway. He was wearing nothing but a hospital gown. He quickly distanced himself from his two pursuers: One was a tall, skinny man in a lab coat; the other a short, heavyset man in an expensive dark suit.

The running man was bleeding profusely from his nose and ears. A throbbing headache temporarily disoriented him, and he crashed into a wall; the hallway reverberated from the impact. Leaving a dented impression he quickly recovered and started running down an adjacent hallway. Its antiseptic smell reminded him of a hospital. As he ran, he searched frantically for an exit. The hallway was long and empty but there was a freight elevator at the far end.

Spotting the elevator, he redoubled his efforts; his body responded, propelling him at a superhuman pace. His speed surprised him but also gave him hope. His feet echoed off the walls as they slapped the cold, tiled floor, drowning out the shouts of his pursuers.

He was fifty feet away when he started crying tears of blood. He was happy. He was relieved. He had finally made it. He was finally free. His white gown was now red down the front. The intensity of his headache made it hard for him to focus but he concentrated on his freedom. He concentrated on seeing the sun again. He concentrated on feeling the wind on his face, and seeing his wife. He had a wife, right? Yes, he did have a wife. And a son. He would see them again… soon. This long nightmare would soon be over.

He was thirty feet away when the elevator doors opened. Three large men in all-black paramilitary gear stepped out. They pointed large semiautomatic rifles at him. He did not stop.

Gunfire erupted.

The bullets ripped through his body. He stopped. His gown was riddled with holes. He swayed back and forth. What was that song he sang to his son?

Hush little baby don't say a word

The muscles on his face twitched. He wondered if he was smiling. And why he was not dead? The fear and revulsion on the gunmen's faces told him they wondered the same thing.

Papa's gonna buy you a mockingbird

The men were holding M16 assault rifles. The banana clips were capable of holding over thirty rounds. How did he know that? Was he a soldier? How long had he been here? His son. He must put his son to bed. He took a step forward.

And if that mockingbird don't sing

Another step; again and again, faster and faster.

Papa's gonna buy you a diamond ring

All three gunmen unloaded their clips into him. He took two steps back. He listened to the song in his head. He remembered how beautiful his wife and son were. His face muscles moved again. He was confident he was smiling this time.

And if that diamond ring don't shine

Taking a final step forward, he collapsed.

Peering around the corner at the body, the skinny man in the lab coat said, "They got him. He's dead." He took out an electronic tablet filled with mathematical formulae. The bullets that ended the life of the subject were of no consequence to him. Judging by his cellular breakdown, the subject had only days left, anyway.

"Well, well, that was extremely unproductive," the large man said, puffing and wheezing.

"So what do we tell them?" asked the skinny man. He mentally assessed the dent the dead man had left on the steel reinforced wall.

"What? What? We tell them we had our second success! Or would have if not for our overzealous rent-a-soldiers."

"But, but... he is... I mean the subject is... he's dead," the skinny man replied, as he watched the armed men reload and cautiously approach the dead subject.

"So? So what? You're the doctor, so you tell me how much strength it would take to break his straps. And you saw how fast the subject moved. If not for these mercs-for-hire killing years of hard work and close to a billion dollars in funding, we would be on our way to committee right now. Now we go with Plan B. Have you located our friend yet?"

Doctor? Hippocratic Oath? He was a long way from that. But there was no going back.

"No...we haven't. But this is what I mentioned in our last meeting." He pointed to a video playing on his electronic tablet.

"Fascinating. Fascinating."

"Look at the history and background," the skinny man instructed, while flipping to a screen of text.

"Interesting. Very interesting. Do we have eyes there?"

"We will within seventy-two hours. And we have a plant starting here." He pointed to a section on the pad.

"Not who… not who I think it is, I hope. That last incident cost us millions in litigation and an immeasurable loss in PR."

"Yes, but I feel that the asset has improved vastly since then." He was trying hard not to be transparent but it was important that his only success get out in the field. That was the only way he would get the recognition he deserved.

"I see. I see. You do realize that these packages are of incalculable value with extremely high profiles. We can't afford any missteps."

"Sir, we have no other option. The other assets are out of the States on assignment."

"Very well. Very well. But this is our highest priority. I want our best assets pulled from their current assignments in the States, and briefed as soon as possible. I want daily reports, and an extraction team on standby, twenty-four-seven."

"Yes, of course."

"Fabulous. Fabulous. Now please clean up down here. It is imperative that we maintain plausible deniability this time."

It's embarrassing how much they pay him, thought the skinny man. He watched the other man waddle off. *And god, I hate the way he talks.*

Chapter 1

"Foul!" shouted Eve, glaring at her younger sister from the ground.

The sun was setting Sunday night over their prestigious upper-class neighborhood, and the three Parker sisters were enjoying one of their favorite pastimes. Playing basketball in the horseshoe driveway of their brick Victorian home was how the sisters spent most of their summer when not traveling. Eve, the oldest of the Parker sisters, was starting ninth grade the next day. She had won four games in a row; she was determined to make it five.

"Please, Princess… that was an offensive charge if anything. Besides, as big as your butt is, I'm surprised you didn't bounce back up." Gwen chuckled as she sauntered off to gather the basketball, roughly tossing it back to Eve.

"Don't even think about fouling me again," Eve hissed. She had been playing basketball for over two hours. She was tired and sweaty and not in the best mood.

"What you going to do, Princess?" Gwen taunted, as she advanced with a sly grin.

"Keep fouling me and you'll find out exactly what I'm going to do!"

"You trying to scare somebody? You better—" Gwen stopped mid-sentence. A flick of Eve's wrist and the basketball bounced off her head.

Eve watched as Gwen's expression fluctuated between grinning and frowning. Frowning won. At five-feet-seven inches, Gwen was two inches shorter than Eve but had a heavier build. She took a threatening step forward.

Eve took a step forward as well, to meet her challenge.

"Ball-in!" Ana—the youngest, thinnest, and tallest sister by two inches—shouted. She threw the ball directly at Eve.

Eve snatched it out of the air. "You ready?"

Gwen nodded, getting in a defensive posture.

Eve started her dribble just as Gwen shouted, "Time!"

"What? Come on, already!" Eve protested.

"That's the second time that cable van has gone by. I think they're up to something."

"Yeah, they are up to something… delivering cable! Stop stalling."

"Delivering cable? On Sunday? Trust me, I have a sixth sense about these things and that truck ain't right!"

"Just like your sixth sense about the ice cream man trying to poison you last year?"

"Innocent misunderstanding."

"You got him arrested and all his ice cream confiscated!"

"Well, he shouldn't have been selling bad ice cream to kids! I was the actual victim!"

"You ate like thirty ice cream sandwiches but the reason you got sick was because they were all bad? Got it. Now let's finish the game!"

"Actually it was thirty-six."

"That's not the point, Ana! The point is, Gwen's stalling because she's scared!"

14

That elicited the desired response from Gwen, who got back in defensive mode. The tension that had momentarily dissipated was back.

Eve judged the distance and angles between her, Gwen, and the basket. She dribbled off to the side to give herself more room to maneuver. Gwen followed while aggressively hand checking her and alternately swiping at the basketball.

"Foul! That's a foul! You can't do that!" Eve's temperature was rising. She switched the ball to her left hand.

"Just shut up and play, Princess," Gwen responded, without getting out of her defensive stance.

Eve slapped Gwen's hand away. She thought about bouncing the ball off Gwen's head again but decided a better punishment would be winning the game. She tried getting past Gwen with a crossover. Gwen didn't fall for it and cut off Eve's path to the basket. Eve reluctantly allowed that Gwen was a great defender. She was strong with quick feet, and enjoyed playing defense in a physical way that intimidated whoever she was up against. But as great a defender as Gwen was, Eve had been blowing past her all day, making layup after layup.

Eve sized Gwen up again, then stutter-stepped, charged, and did a spin move to get around her. Coming out of her spin, Eve lost her balance when Gwen swiped at the ball. Abruptly Eve felt a tingling in her stomach, and she was filled with a burning sensation, like there was a fire inside of her.

What is going on? She thought. The ball was suspended in mid-air. Gwen was frozen in place. Eve blinked. Both the ball and Gwen slowly started moving again. Regaining her balance and control of the ball, she easily avoided Gwen. Three steps and she was at the rim, when everything returned to normal speed. She bricked a layup.

Ana retrieved the rebound. She dribbled to the section of the driveway marked for three pointers, and launched a jumper. The ball went through, hitting nothing but the bottom of the net.

"I believe that is game," Ana stated casually.

No one said anything else as the ball rolled slowly down the driveway, into the middle of the street, and back to the curb. Eve was clutching her chest. Her heart was beating so fast and hard it was painful. Dripping with sweat, she bent to over to catch her breath while rubbing her chest. A minute went by with Ana and Gwen staring intently at their sister.

Gwen broke the silence. "OK...what was that?"

"I... I don't know. I am not sure what happened," Eve responded between deep breaths.

"You're smoking!"

"What? You know I don't smoke!"

Ana pointed at Eve's arms, "She is referring to the steam that is coming off your body."

"Told ya you were smoking. But you haven't answered the question—how did you do it? You were like a blur."

"I said I don't know! All I know is I'm tired and I'm going in." Eve started for the door.

"Wait! You promised to work with me on my crossover!"

"Gwen, we'll do it tomorrow. I promise. I'm just too tired right now."

16

"Yeah, like you've been promising all summer. Go get your hair done, Princess. I don't need your help!"

Eve turned around and eyed Gwen, who ignored her as she retrieved the ball. Eve opened her mouth to say something but closed it again and continued into the house.

Once inside, Eve shut the door behind her. Holding her arms out, she noted they were now dry. Grabbing a large water bottle out of the fridge, Eve headed upstairs to her bedroom. She replayed the sequence over and over in her head, getting more and more confused. Taking another sip of the water, she noticed blood on the floor and realized her nose was bleeding.

***

"Eve, so, do you want to talk about it now?" Gwen asked the next morning, as they sat down to eat at their marble top breakfast bar. The breakfast bar was in the center of an expansive gourmet kitchen that was bathed in natural light from the oversized screen doors and windows that faced an equally oversized and meticulously manicured lawn.

Eve looked up from her book. "Talk about what? I still don't know what happened. I stayed up all night looking up stuff on the Internet for clues, but I couldn't find anything."

Gwen, her mouth full, looked up from her bowl of cereal. "Are you going to tell Mom and Dad? Maybe you should go to the doctor?"

"No! Absolutely not! Whatever it is I'll work it out myself, and I don't want you or Ana to say anything either. All I want to do now is get through this first week of school while I try to figure this out."

"Oh right… God forbid you stay home on the first day of school and ruin your perfect reputation. And don't even think about trying to get out of Tae Kwon Do practice this Saturday. It's been four weeks and Dad is complaining about wasting money again."

"Don't worry, I'll be more than happy to apply your weekly beat down." Eve laughed while studying her hair and face in a compact mirror.

"Say what? Your pitty-patty kicks don't do anything but tickle me. Besides, you know you can't fight with a mirror in your hand, right?"

"Don't hate! I can't help it if I'm a beautiful, intelligent, strong woman."

"Pleeeeease! You're a snobby, self-absorbed bookworm with anger management issues!" laughed Gwen.

"The disproportionate amount of time you spend on appearance could indicate an unhealthy level of narcissism," chimed in Ana, as she furiously typed away on a laptop.

"Aren't you banned from laptops? And speaking of narcissism, how long did you spend styling your afro puffs this morning? And Gwen, I have never seen a person spend more time and energy picking out clothes that are intended to give the impression that one doesn't care about one's appearance. At least I'm honest."

"Well, Eve, unlike some my sartorial style is intended to give the impression that I am not a conformist and will not abide by societal rules or norms on how I should dress. I have consciously chosen the path less traveled. Furthermore—" Ana responded, before being interrupted by Gwen.

"Oh my god! You're killing me! 'Path less traveled?' That wouldn't be the path for dorks, would it? Listen, dressing like a clown doesn't give you the right to spout obscure sayings from a TV commercial. And why are you on the laptop? Are you pirating games again? Why don't you do something useful like figure out what is going on with Eve?"

"Of course, I have some theories on what is going on with Eve. But that's all they are at this point and inasmuch would serve no purpose sharing without further research. And for your information I never 'technically' pirated any games. Besides, I have moved on to more lucrative ventures. Plus—"

"Listen, Band Geek, the only thing you need to be doing is finding out what is going on with Eve and seeing if anyone on our street got cable delivered yesterday. Capisce?"

"Orchestra! I'm in orchestra and you are not an authority figure, so you can't tell me what to do!"

"Orchestra, dork-estra. And I'm going to need you to front me a little extra change for lunch this week before Mom and Dad find out about your 'lucrative ventures,' or would you rather I make you go out for track?"

"Band is wind instruments! Orchestra is string instruments! And please, listen carefully because this is the last time I am going to say this... I am never, ever running track. Running around a big oval serves no functional purpose on top of being just silly."

19

From a large clip that she pulled from her pocket, Ana placed two twenty bills in Gwen's outstretched hand.

Their parents came down together. Their mother, a tall woman, had the skin tone of lightly toasted bread, and was sharply dressed in a black business suit-dress

"Hurry up! You're going to be late! Ana, I saw you on that laptop!" she cried out, after kissing Barry, their father. Barry wiped his tortoise shell glasses on his blue button-down shirt and helped usher the girls out of the kitchen. Eve kissed her father before leaving, while thinking she had the worst of both worlds: She had her father's dark chocolate skin tone while her sisters' complexion mirrored their mother's. Yet she had her mother's body type, which consisted of big legs and hips. Ana was skinny as a beanpole and Gwen, although muscular for a girl, had a more balanced build.

The Parker sisters attended a small middle school tucked away in one of the richest suburbs in the state. The school was consistently ranked as one of the top academic schools in the nation. It shared its parking lot and sport fields with its sister high school located on the adjoining block.

Eve stepped out the car, rubbing her temples. She had a throbbing headache and, although she'd not had shin splints since her first year running track, she had them that morning. Also, every muscle in her body was sore, making every movement painful. To top it off, Eve was not happy with her hair. Her mother had attempted to hot comb it the night before but her hair remained defiant. So instead of having straight, silky hair she was forced to sport a natural with a pink ribbon. *No matter,* she thought, while forcing her hand away from her hair and heading for the school entrance.

Great! Eve thought when she saw Amy outside the school doors. As usual, Amy was surrounded by a cadre of admirers and friends. At six feet tall, Amy was a head taller than everyone around her except Lucia, who was just as tall as Amy but twice as wide. And as usual, Amy was killing it in a beautiful blue sleeveless dress that showed off her svelte figure and toned arms.

Eve almost stopped in her tracks when she realized that, to enter school, she had to walk past Amy and her entourage. As she casually glanced around for an alternative route, she noticed Amy looking directly at her. Without breaking her stride, Eve held her head up high and continued on her original path.

As she got closer, the talk stopped. She could feel everyone looking at her. Looking straight ahead, she focused on the door and prayed she didn't stumble.

"Hey, Eve," Lucia said, as Eve walked past.

"Oh, hey, Lucia." Eve attempted to sound surprised, but immediately regretted it.

"Hey, Eve, how was your summer? Didn't see you or Gwen at any track meets," Amy added.

"Hello, Amy. We didn't run this summer. We spent a lot of time in the city visiting our great grandmother." Eve tried not to look at Amy's long, blonde hair and smooth, tanned skin.

Amy leaned in and whispered, "Yeah, Kang mentioned something about that. I hope she's doing better."

"She was. I mean she's going to be fine."

"Great. I'm glad. And I think the team is going to be really good this year! I can't wait to get on the court!"

"This is our year!" Lucia added, shaking her with fist with an intensity that forced her long, braided ponytails to whip from side to side. It almost made Eve smile.

"I agree. This year can be special. Well, I guess I better head in. Bye Lucia, bye Amy."

As Eve walked away, the whispers started. She fought against quickening her pace. Amy and Eve had always had a cool relationship. Last year was the first year they were on the same team after competing against each other fiercely the previous five years in basketball and track. Amy almost always won those competitions. But this was Eve's year, so she had to figure out what had happened yesterday and put it behind her before anyone else found out. She planned on dominating Amy and everyone else, and didn't want to leave any doubt as to who was the best… at everything.

***

Gwen waited until her mother drove off before rolling up the left sleeve of her football jersey to show off her muscular arm. While scanning the crowd she tilted her baseball cap to the side and made sure her French braids poked out the back.

"Hey Gwen, Gwen!" shouted Melissa, while running up and hugging her. Melissa and Gwen had been best friends since third grade. She was short and wiry with long, curly red hair. Her bright freckles practically jumped off her face and her smiling, emerald eyes always seemed like they were hiding something.

"Missy!" Gwen caught her in a bear hug.

"OK! OK! Put me down! Jeez, you got stronger. Hey, did you see Antonio this summer? He is so gorgeous! Did you tell him my soccer team made it to the regionals? I am so going to marry him, watch!"

"Girl, Antonio ain't thinking about you!" Gwen laughed.

"You know, I called and texted you like a million times last week. What's the deal?"

"Me and the Princess got into another argument. This time we broke both of our phones, a couple of chairs, and a window. Mom and Dad hit the roof. We were banned from the Internet and they said we're never getting phones again."

"Bummer. But if it was anything like the argument you two had at basketball practice last year, I'm sorry I missed it. Man oh man, that was awesome! You and Eve got some serious moves!" Melissa started shadow boxing.

"Girl, you need to stop!"

"You know I'm right!" Melissa added, laughing. "And hey, if it wasn't for that frog thing we probably could have some classes together! I'm so bummed!"

Gwen doubled over laughing. "We don't have any classes together this year because the baseball team is a bunch of crybabies!"

"Oh my God! That was hilarious! I did feel sorry for Javier, though! He was so gorgeous with all that hair! If your cousin Antonio doesn't wise up I might have to bring Javier in off the bench!"

23

"Girl, you delusional!" Gwen laughed. She and Melissa linked arms and walked into school together, laughing and giggling all the way.

"Hey, Shorty, whaddup?" Kang playfully punched Gwen in the arm and blocked her path to the cafeteria. "How come you haven't been at Tae Kwon Do, lately? My uncle keeps asking about you."

Gwen looked up at Kang towering over her with his muscular build and flattop Mohawk. Her friends started to giggle and Gwen admitted that Kang was fine. His chiseled features and full lips made her forget he'd asked her a question.

"Well, if it ain't the Gwenster!" Tyler walked up and stood next to Kang. His interruption allowed Gwen to refocus. She smirked at Tyler, who was taller and thinner than Kang but more than his match in the looks department. "You and your girls coming to the game this week? Y'all know we playing Lincoln?"

"I would love to watch you guys get smashed. Unfortunately, I have a life so I'll have to check my schedule and get back to you," laughed Gwen.

"Hey, Kang, can't speak?" Toni teased, as she pulled up next to Gwen. Gwen watched as Kang breathed in Toni's appearance. Toni was almost as tall as Kang in her Manolo Blahniks. It was easy for Gwen to identify the high-end shoe. She had a fashionista for a sister and had once used her mother's Manolo Blahniks to crack open walnuts. She hadn't been able to sit down for a week.

"Toni, you know we besties." Kang smiled as he lifted Toni off her feet with a hug. Toni possessed a confident, flirty nature that the boys loved and the girls envied. Her appearance didn't hurt either, with her spiked blonde hair, lithe build, and smiling blue eyes.

Too many damn beautiful people in this school! Gwen thought. *Between Toni, Amy, and Eve, the rest of us are going to be left dating the chess team!*

"What it is, Gwen? You and your crew coming or not? Y'all know me and Kang going to be in straight beast mode!" Tyler said, smiling and revealing his hypnotic dimples of death. He turned his head sideways and comically patted his enormous afro like he was mugging for a camera.

"Does beast mode now mean dropping passes and getting sacked?" Gwen laughed.

"Ah, so you got jokes! I gotta run but come to the game and bring Eve. Let's roll, Kang!" Tyler turned and ran off.

"That boy is going to hurt somebody with them dimples!" Toni whispered to Gwen as they watched Tyler run down the hall.

"Gwen, I heard about you and Bob, so call me if you want to work on some counters or angles or something," Kang said seriously, putting a hand on Gwen's shoulder before turning and running after Tyler. "Yo, dawg! Wait up!"

"So what do you think?" Gwen asked, as she sat down at one end of the most crowded table in the cafeteria. The eclectic group of students made room for Gwen and her three friends.

"Seriously? We talking about the new girl? The girl with the long, frizzy hair who dresses like she goes to Hogwarts?" Toni replied.

Toni was right; the new girl was frumpy, but everyone was kind of frumpy compared to Toni. Gwen inspected her out the corner of eye: Her designer jeans were so tight it was a wonder she could sit down; her Ramones t-shirt was a nice touch, but the large diamond earrings were what stood out. And the diamonds were real. In a school full of rich kids, Toni was one of the richest.

"Anyway," Gwen continued, "she's the tallest girl in the school and she does have some experience. Check it...put her at center, Lucia slides to power forward, Amy slides to small forward, with me and Eve at the guards...can somebody say championship?"

"Girl, you crazy if you think Hermione is going to help us win a championship!" laughed Toni.

Gwen shrugged her shoulders as she started shoveling food in her mouth. Her already healthy appetite had increased exponentially the last month, and Gwen could not stop eating.

"Gwen, how can you eat so much and not gain weight?" Rebecca brushed her untamed hair out of her eyes and looked down at her own stout frame, adding, "It's not fair."

"I hab a high me-tab-bo-ism." Gwen struggled to say with a mouth full of food.

"The new girl's name is Elizabeth. I've done piano competitions with her. She's really good," Dana said.

"As good as you?" inquired Toni.

"Better. The few times I've seen her she finished in the top three."

"Javier is looking over here again. How did you and Melissa get away with that, Gwen?" Rebecca asked, while holding her hand over her mouth to cover her braces.

"Get away with what? I have absolutely no idea what you're talking about."

"Oh yeah? Then how come your grandmother's law firm donated a new batting cage and new uniforms to the team?" chuckled Toni.

"Our baseball team sucks. I'm sure my grandmother hoped that her magnanimous gesture might spur them to a winning season. Sadly, she was mistaken."

"You know you and Melissa put that hair remover in the boys' showers last year. Just like you and her let all those frogs loose in the cafeteria," laughed Toni.

"Well, I think Javier needed to be taken down a notch. He thinks he so cool because his dad played professional baseball and is always on TV," Rebecca said, looking up from her plate and covering her braces again.

Toni nodded in the direction of Javier's table. "He told me and Dana that he might check out our cross country meet this weekend, if he isn't too busy with football. And I was like, spare me, Casanova; if you spent as much time practicing as hitting on me you might actually win a game this year." Dana laughed so hard at Toni's comment she drew stares. Her long, curled black hair bounced up and down as she nodded in agreement. Her bronze skin was practically radiating and she didn't seem to mind the extra attention.

27

"Would milady fancy another cupcake?" interrupted Eric—a small, pale, seventh grade gamer—as he passed a cupcake down the table.

Gwen nodded and reached for the cupcake when her hand seized, forcing her to drop it.

Toni placed the cupcake on Gwen's tray and looked directly at her. "You alright?"

Gwen was silent. She closed her eyes and tried to wish the pain away. When she opened them, her hand was numb. She shook it, trying to get the feeling back, before massaging it with her other hand.

"Gwen?" Toni persisted, still staring at her.

Gwen shrugged. "I'm good. I'm cool. Just been having these crazy muscle spasms the last few weeks."

"Uh huh," Toni replied, not sounding convinced.

Gwen glanced around and wiped the sweat from her brow. A table full of friends and the only ones who noticed her pain were Toni and Eric. Her appetite gone, she forced herself to eat the cupcake. She wondered what was happening to her, whether it was related to what Eve experienced yesterday. She wondered about the suspicious van she saw. Gwen was still perspiring as she stood to put her tray away. She wiped her brow but again, no one noticed except Toni, Eric, and the school's new security guard.

***

Ana watched Eve and Gwen go off in separate directions. She carefully adjusted her two large afro puffs to ensure they were symmetrical. They resembled Mickey Mouse ears, as she was told by everyone, but she refused to part with them. She then checked that the rolled up sleeves on her pink-and-green plaid shirt were even. The shirt was in stark contrast with her orange capri pants and black-and-yellow polka dot socks, which themselves were in stark contrast to her mismatched tennis shoes: one red, one purple.

Wardrobe check completed, Ana stared at a leaf on one of the trees that surrounded the campus, and attempted to reconcile what Eve had done yesterday with what she knew of the human body. *And how did heat factor into the equation?* Ana pondered.

"Ana! Ana! Ana!" yelled Stacey, in rapid succession. Stacey moved as fast as her plump legs would carry her, stressing the elasticity of her miniskirt. Out of breath, she reached up to hurriedly hug Ana. Her curly blonde hair brushed Ana's nose, almost making her sneeze.

Fanning herself with one hand and shaking her sweaty blouse with the other, she began the onslaught.

"Missed you so much over the summer. What did you do? My mother sent me to a fat camp which is just crazy, right? Look, there's Maddy! Maddy! Maddy! Oh my God! It's the first day of school and she has her viola! She is going to be first chair again and make us look bad! Hey, Maddy! How was your summer? Ana, your sister is crazy! Everyone is talking about the bike on the roof stunt. Oh, and I heard that Tyler likes Eve! I mean, we are talking about Tyler! One word: awesome! Wouldn't they make the cutest couple! We are going to have so much fun in orchestra this year! Oh, I almost forgot, my mother says that if I watch my diet I can get a horse! And the place where I take my horseback-riding lessons is going to let us board him there. Isn't that exciting! Ana, look at all the students! We are going to make so much money this year!"

Stacey's incessant chatter continued unabated as the three friends entered school. Maddy and Ana nodded and smiled. Ana could tell them at a later date that she would not be joining them in selling candy this year. Ana had moved on to bigger and better things—she had dreams of making a fortune to rival her grandmother's, and selling candy in the hallways and bathrooms did not factor into that equation. She just had to wait for the right moment to break it to her friends.

Ana's last class of the day was math. Having heard that the new math teacher was cool and handsome, Ana was actually looking forward to it. Not that she actually planned on putting forth any effort in math, or any other class for that matter. Ana seldom did well in school and she had too much on her plate to change that now. Besides, if she brought home an A her parents might have a heart attack, so her consistently underperforming was in their best interest.

The math teacher's name was Mr. Little. Ana thought he looked young for a teacher. He was of medium height and his shiny mane of curly brown hair fell to his shoulders. His motorcycle helmet was prominently displayed on his desk. His introduction to class revealed sparkling white teeth, and he had the type of three o'clock shadow that every hero wears in every cheap action movie.

Taking roll call, Mr. Little paused when he got to Ana's name. "Ana Parker?"

"Yes," Ana replied, without looking up.

"Ms. Parker, I expect you to look at me when I'm speaking with you," Mr. Little said coldly.

"Apologies." Ana was surprised. She wasn't intentionally being disrespectful but was just tired, and she had a throbbing headache from not sleeping the night before.

"Thank you, Ms. Parker... now, you wouldn't be the granddaughter of Josephine Jefferson-Harris, would you?"

"I would."

"Very good, Ms. Parker. Well, I'm a huge fan of your grandmother and I would accept nothing but the very best from you in my class. Is that understood?"

"It is." Being the granddaughter of a billionaire civil rights icon, and president and majority owner of the most powerful privately held law firm in the country, always garnered Ana and her sisters unwanted attention. Having grown up in their grandmother's orbit, they were accustomed to the attention, if not fond of it.

As Ana packed up to leave, she noticed that Mr. Little was watching her closely. Ana was not overly concerned—she and her sisters had developed defense mechanisms to handle overenthusiastic teachers and classmates. Plus, Ana had big plans for the year and she would not be assuaged by a celebrity-chasing teacher with too much mousse in his hair.

Chapter 2

"Sit down!" Master Kim, a diminutive, older South Korean with weathered skin and a thick head of graying hair, spoke sharply to Ana and Maddy. It had been four weeks since the start of school and over two months since the Parker girls had been to Tae Kwon Do. The Tae Kwon Do area was encased in a glass room and located inside a large fitness center that was itself located in an upscale strip mall fifteen minute drive from their house. For Eve, the smells of the mats mixed with perspiration brought back fond memories. She was happy to be back.

She shook her head disapprovingly at Ana, who yawned and ignored her while sitting down. Ana and Madhuri (or Maddy, as Ana called her), had just spent the last minute circling each other but refusing to engage. Ana should have dominated. They were both red belts, both rail thin—although Ana was taller—but unlike Maddy, Ana was a great fighter. Problem was, she never attacked. The other students knew this and never engaged Ana. And as good as Ana was, Eve didn't know why she refused to take the black belt test. Eve and Gwen had been black belts for two years and hoped to test for their second degree stripe the following month. Ana seemed content to be a red belt for the rest of her life.

"Eve," Master Kim said in a steady, measured tone. Eve jumped up quickly. She loved this. Sparring allowed her to excel in a medium she was great at, and unlike in basketball, she didn't have to worry about teammates holding her back.

As Master Kim surveyed the class, everyone except Gwen looked preoccupied.

"Manesh!" Master Kim finally said.

Manesh got up slowly. Manesh was Madhuri's older brother and the largest student in class. He was a tall, boxy, built tenth grader who towered over Eve. He, however, did not look confident about his prospects.

"Fight!" Master Kim shouted. Eve started bouncing and felt the best she'd felt in weeks. Her mind cleared of distractions. She gauged Manesh's reaction time by throwing feints. The last time they'd sparred, she had handily beaten him by using her speed to mitigate his length. His timing calculated, Eve attacked. She jumped right. Manesh pivoted to face her. She slid in and scored three kicks. As Manesh reset to counter, Eve jumped left and stepped out. She was out of his range when Manesh badly missed with his kick.

The class cheered. Eve smiled. Her execution was flawless. She calmly waited for Manesh's attack. A second later, Manesh rushed in and threw a clumsy kick. Still smiling, Eve thought, *Perfect!* She could not have choreographed it better herself. She timed her spinning back kick perfectly. Manesh's leg was fully extended when Eve's kick connected with his sternum—the impact knocked him on his butt. He landed hard with a loud thump.

The class erupted.

This is what I need, Eve thought to herself, as she reset at the center of the circle. The loud clapping and cheering rejuvenated her. A second later, she was joined by a visibly embarrassed Manesh.

Master Kim yelled, "Fight!" Manesh took an imposing step and launched a roundhouse kick. Eve was caught off guard. She gritted her teeth and blocked down, bracing for impact. Unexpectedly, she felt a tingling in the pit of her stomach. She knew what was happening. The heat followed, although it was not as intense as the first time. Manesh's foot stopped before it connected. Stepping back, Eve realized it was not Manesh, but her. She was moving at a super-speed, a speed so fast that everything appeared frozen. Manesh did a full turn when his foot hit nothing but air. He lost his balance and again landed on his butt.

The room was quiet. A wisp of steam escaped from Eve's uniform and glided lazily toward the ceiling. Panting, Eve closely watched the other students. Turning from side to side the students looked at each other with mouths agape. Even Master Kim was speechless. Eve locked eyes with Gwen, who gave a subtle nod before she started energetically clapping and whistling. The other students joined. The noise reached a crescendo before Master Kim was able to quiet everyone down.

Eve felt a jumble of emotions and thoughts as she sat down, as instructed by Master Kim. Ana assisted Eve with taking off her sparring equipment. Neither said a word.

"Gwen, Bob." Master Kim said. The class went quiet. No two students detested each other more than Gwen and Bob. Despite the differences in size and age, they were also two of the strongest kickers. Bob, in tenth grade, was the second largest student in class. He utilized a similar style to Gwen's, which consisted of standing flat footed and delivering powerful kicks. In their last match, Gwen had experienced some success by timing Bob's kicks and getting on the inside. The match before that, Bob had dominated her.

Eve watched as Bob circled Gwen. He threw feints that Gwen didn't bite on. Bob was employing a new strategy; he was attempting to limit his exchanges with Gwen. Eve started yelling instructions to Gwen. The Booger twins started yelling and cheering for Gwen as well.

After slowly circling to his left, he jumped to his right. Gwen pivoted to face him. Bob jumped in, landing a kick to Gwen's padded torso which she partially blocked. She attempted to counter, but Bob jumped out of range.

"Come on, Gwen! Bounce! Get on your toes!" Eve shouted.

Gwen started to bounce on her toes.

"That's it, Gwen! You got this!" Eve continued, while pounding the mat with both hands. She was joined by the other students.

Bob switched his stance. Eve noticed he was favoring his kicking foot. Unless he switched back he was going to attack with his left.

"Gwen! Switch feet! Switch feet!" Eve yelled. Gwen complied in time to block a slower kick from Bob. Bouncing on her toes, she quickly countered.

Bob blocked down. His arm ricocheted off her foot. A snap was heard. The trajectory of Gwen's kick was unchanged—it landed on the padded area beneath his armpit. The impact sent him airborne, and he landed four feet away, immediately curling into the fetal position and crying in pain.

Everyone was up shouting and screaming. The only people who remained silent were Eve, Ana, and Gwen.

***

The paramedics told Master Kim that Bob had suffered a broken arm and bruised rib cage. Gwen, visibly upset, was being consoled by the rest of the class.

The ride home was silent. Eve stared at the houses and buildings going by without seeing any of them. She understood something of what had happened to her today and a few weeks ago. It was similar to an adrenaline rush, but magnified. This magnified adrenaline rush allowed her to move at a super speed for a second or two. But her body was not accustomed to operating at that speed. That would explain her elevated heart rate, profuse sweating, shin splints, and sore muscles. And it was obvious that Gwen was stronger than normal. And now, because of Eve's selfish silence, Bob was on his way to the hospital. Eve must come clean now. She had to, or the next incident might be more serious than broken bones.

***

"Hello! I'm home!" Michelle shouted, throwing open the front door. Her mother's driver, Mr. Brown, helped her with the luggage.

Barry and the girls came down the hallway from the kitchen to greet her.

"Mr. Parker, good to see you again, sir," Mr. Brown said to Barry in a stiff and formal tone.

"Thanks, Nino, it's good to see you too."

"Nino, we have it from here. Thanks," Michelle said.

"As you wish, Mrs. Parker," Mr. Brown said, tipping his hat and avoiding everyone on his way out. *Mr. Brown is a strange character* Michelle thought. He served as her mother's driver, pilot, and security guard, and her mother trusted him unequivocally. He had been with her over five years after serving a decade in Special Forces and thirteen years in the Secret Service. But his always jittery bloodshot eyes, coal-black skin, and a frame that could best be described as gaunt, more closely resembled a ghostly specter than it did a substantive human being. Michelle was always on edge in his presence.

"OK, girls, let me take a shower and I'll be down with your gifts," Michelle said, heading upstairs with a suitcase. Barry followed with her two other large suitcases.

All Michelle wanted to do was take a shower, pour a large glass of wine, and go to bed. But there was absolutely no way the girls would let her sleep without receiving their gifts first. And by Barry's body language, Michelle deduced he knew about her job situation—a development she should have shared before she left for France.

"Barry?"

"Yes."

"We need to talk."

"I know, Michelle. I know. It's just that—"

"Barry, everything is going to be OK. The acquisition isn't finalized and I already put out some feelers. I know the financial sector isn't what it used to be, but with my résumé I'm sure I can find something. And that's not even factoring in any severance." Michelle knew Barry was too proud to accept any financial assistance from her mother. He always had been. But with her severance and their savings they should be OK for a while. Worst case scenario would be they'd dip into their 401(k), until they got through this.

"Acquisition?"

"Yes. There is talk of my firm being acquired. Isn't that what's bothering you?"

"Michelle, we need to talk about the girls."

"What about the girls?"

"Gwen hurt a kid today in sparring."

"I thought Gwen only sparred with boys now? Is the kid OK? Who was it?" Gwen hurting someone while sparring was old news. Tae Kwon Do sparring was based on points, but Gwen seemed to think she was doing MMA.

"Robert. She hurt Robert." Barry stumbled over his words.

"That child is twice her size. Is it serious? Is he going to be OK?"

Barry filled Michelle in on the incidents earlier that day.

Michelle sat down on the bed and didn't respond.

"Michelle?"

"So, Gwen hurt a kid and you made her come home and lift weights after you weighed her? And Eve disappeared or something?"

"No, Eve did not disappear. She just moves faster than the eye can follow, or so she says. And I had to see how strong Gwen is; plus she's a lot bigger than she looks."

Michelle got up to pace without looking at Barry. Abruptly, she left the bedroom. "Girls! Meet me in the basement. Now!"

A short while later the family is in the basement while Michelle skeptically eyes Gwen, "OK, Gwen, let's see what you can do, but be careful, that's a lot of weight. Barry, make sure my baby doesn't get hurt," Michelle instructed, still in disbelief that she'd actually seen Gwen tip the scales at 198 lbs.

Barry nodded and positioned himself in a spotter position at the head of the bench.

Michelle held her breath. Barry said the weight and bar came to 225 lbs, an unsupportable weight for a young child.

Gwen smiled, gave her a thumbs up, laid down, and started benching the weight with a steady rhythm. She got to eighteen reps before noticeably straining. At twenty-two she began to struggle. Twenty-five barely went up. She held the weight steady for a few seconds and took two deep breaths, and twenty-six went up. Two more deep breaths: twenty-seven went up. Two more deep breaths, the weight went down and got half way up before stopping. Slowly it started going back down. Gwen was grunting and straining with everything she had, but to no avail.

With the assistance of her father Gwen was able to rack it. Both Barry and Gwen were exhausted by the effort.

Sitting back up, Gwen folded her arms and smiled from ear to ear.

"Gwen, that is amazing! That has to be a world record for a girl your age—" Michelle exclaimed. "Oh, look dear, your nose is bleeding." Michelle wiped Gwen's bleeding with a handkerchief then tilted her head back and applied pressure. "Now, Eve, can you tell me what happened with you today?"

Eve looked at everyone before starting, "I was blocking Manesh's kick when I felt a tingling in my stomach followed by an intense heat."

"What happened after that?" Michelle pressed.

"Everything stopped moving. Or rather, everything appeared to stop moving. I think I was just moving really fast. Everything then gradually started to move again until it got back to normal speed."

"It was incredible!" shouted Gwen, "Eve was like a blur! Manesh was about to kick her and then swoosh! She was gone and he completely missed! It was the coolest thing I've ever seen."

Ana nodded in agreement. "It was interesting, to say the least; it seems her sympathetic nervous system is performing at a superhuman level."

"Say what?"

"Her fight or flight response has increased exponentially. Or, in short, she becomes really fast under duress," Ana answered.

"Anyway... it was superfast. You couldn't even see it. Mom, you should have been there and seen the look on Master Kim's face! It was hilarious!"

"Afterwards, I was spent... my muscles stiffened up and everything. I couldn't even catch my breath."

"Hmm, OK, girls—is there anything we should know about, or anything else you would like to share?"

"Well, this is the second time this speed thing, or whatever you want to call it, has happened. The first time was the Sunday before the first day of school. I made Ana and Gwen promise not to say anything. I thought I could figure it out myself... I thought it would go away."

"I see... Gwen, Ana, would you like to share anything?"

"Well, I guess, I mean...I have to use toenail clippers for my fingernails. Regular clippers don't work anymore."

"Let me have a look."

Gwen, nose no longer bleeding, stood up with fingers extended and palms down. Michelle examined Gwen's finger nails. What she noticed were abnormally dense fingernails that had been crudely cut.

"You do have exceptionally strong and thick fingernails. I'll trim them until we see what the doctor says. OK?"

"What about my hair? Can I get extensions like Aunt Zora?"

"Eve, you know this family does not do synthetic hair, but when I was in Paris I saw some fabulous natural styles that I can't wait to try on you."

"Natural?" Eve sounded unconvinced.

"Child, you will be fine!" Michelle laughed, hugging Eve. "Oh, my... you are a bit warm. I better take your temperature. How do you feel?"

"I feel fine."

"I wouldn't be alarmed if Eve's temperature is outside the norm. Her core is probably running higher than normal so an elevated temperature should be expected," Ana lectured.

41

"Nevertheless, I am taking her temperature. After which your father and I will have a discussion on what to do next. OK, girls, is that all? Is there anything else we should know?"

"Well, isn't it obvious, Mother?"

"Isn't what obvious, Ana?"

"Look at Gwen. She looks like a normal thirteen-year-old girl who doesn't weigh much more than a hundred pounds. But she weighs almost two hundred pounds! So she must be extremely dense to pack all that muscle in a relatively small space. And, as strong as she is now, she is going to get a lot stronger if her fingernails are any indication."

"I'm sorry, dear, but what is so special about her fingernails?"

"Fingernails are made of keratin and not bone; however, there's a strong correlation between the density of fingernails and bones. I hypothesize that Gwen is going to get significantly stronger! And her body knows this. Her bones are getting stronger so they won't break from the stress they will be under from all the weight Gwen will be able to eventually lift," Ana said authoritatively, while crossing her arms.

"Say what? How cool is that! Everybody say it with me—who's awesome and getting awesomer by the minute?" Gwen shouted.

Michelle smiled as she led Barry back upstairs.

"We need to take the girls to a specialist right away. Ana was right, Eve's temperature is elevated. And what Gwen just did was absolutely amazing!"

Barry did not respond as he closed the door behind him.

"Maybe a scientist or someone in sports medicine? Maybe my cousin? What do you think?"

"We cannot tell anyone about this. At least not until you know everything," a downcast Barry said.

"Excuse me?" Michelle stood up, hands on her hips.

"You remember my friend David Hamilton?"

"Yes, I remember David. The physicist, right? I thought you hadn't heard from him since that explosion?"

"I haven't, but—"

Michelle interrupted him before he could finish. "Well, what does he have to do with Gwen weighing almost two hundred pounds and Eve being lightning-quick?"

"Well, that's what I am getting at… He, uh, operated on me."

"Excuse me? It must be the acoustics in here, but it sounded like you said he operated on you?"

"Yes. The operation was supposed to increase the probability of us having a son. And—"

"But he's a physicist! Not a medical doctor, and—"

"I know, I know, but he is the smartest person I know, and—"

"I don't doubt he's the smartest person you know! He's a physicist! And even if he were a medical doctor there is no such operation!" Michelle was now pacing, while Barry stayed rooted.

"Yeah, well, he said he could put some type of smart device in me that would release an enzyme or protein or something that limited the production of XX chromosomes—"

"OK, I got it! And not only did you believe that nonsense, but you allowed him? You allowed this mad scientist to insert something into you?"

"Well... the night before we left Vegas I'd been drinking a lot. He kept badgering me about it and I finally relented. The realization didn't even hit until I was on the plane home the next day. By then it was too late. I wasn't able to contact him for another five years."

"This is starting to sound like a bad movie. You actually got drunk in Vegas and let your college buddy operate on you? So you could have a son?"

"Michelle, please. It's not like that! I was just—"

"What's it like, Barry? You know, in less developed countries the birth of a male baby is considered a blessing due to the second-class status given to females of these supposedly inferior cultures. Some parents even practice female infanticide to preserve the family honor and avoid paying a dowry. Here in the States, I thought we were enlightened! But no, not us! The only difference between us and them is access to technology! Was it worth it, Barry? Look at our little girls now and tell me it was worth it?"

"I got it! I know! But what can I do now! If I could go back I would!"

"OK...this device?"

"Well it's out now, but I think it must have mutated the DNA in my chromosomes or something—"

"You think?"

"Will you please let me finish?" Barry blinked. "Thank you! David stole equipment to do it! Alright? I'm an accessory to a felony!"

"Seriously? That did not raise any flags for you? I don't think this David character is being completely straight with you."

"OK, OK, I, but… now we need to decide what to do. And we need to do it together. I have no problem doing the right thing, but we decide this together."

"Barry, I—I can't believe you did this to us! To our family! How could you?" Michelle actually felt her hands shaking. She attempted to slow her breathing and calm her nerves. This was not how Michelle usually reacted under stress; she was normally more pragmatic than emotional. Putting a hand to her head, she closed her eyes. "I need some time."

"Well, let me know when you're ready to talk about this like adults," Barry said, leaving the room.

Oh, so now he wants to play the adult card? Michelle was incredulous. An hour ago she thought the biggest issue the Parker family faced was financial. Now her most pressing matter was finding out what was going on with her daughters without sending her husband to jail. And she had to be discreet enough to not let her press-averse mother find out. Michelle left the bedroom, and returned shortly with a wine bottle and a large goblet of wine.

Her uncle and cousin were doctors, but there was no way Michelle could involve them now.

Sitting down on the bed she finished her second glass. No child should be required to keep a secret of this magnitude. The stress her daughters were under must be overwhelming. Michelle took consolation from the fact that at least Ana had been unaffected by Barry's harebrained scheme. She poured herself another glass as she struggled with what they had to do. She didn't like it, but there was one option that could be done discreetly. And the sooner they acted the better.

Chapter 3

"Ana, how did you get two million dollars in your account?" Barry had Michelle at his side and he was not pleased. He'd received a call from the bank informing him that two million dollars had been transferred to the account of an Anastasia Parker, of which he and Mrs. Parker were the primaries.

This was something the family did not need. They had taken some comfort in the fact that Ana had escaped any adverse effects from his and Dave's experiment. But if the bank was correct their comfort was only temporary.

"Excuse me?" replied Ana, as she looked up from the breakfast bar.

"Where did this money come from?" Michelle chimed in.

"What money?"

"The two million in your checking account." Barry tapped his foot and wiped his glasses on his shirt.

"Oh that money… I made it by trading stocks."

"You expect us to believe that you made two million by trading stocks?" Michelle asked.

"Actually I made about twenty-nine million. I must have accidently transferred two million into my personal checking instead of my payroll account. My bad."

"OK, I'll bite… how did you make twenty-nine million dollars selling stock?" Barry cleaned his glasses again and forced himself to stop tapping his foot. He knew enough already. Ana had been more secretive than usual as of late, and he knew she had not been getting much sleep. No matter what time he walked past her bedroom door a light was on.

"By speed trading."

"What is speed trading?"

"It's also known as high frequency trading. It's big on Wall Street. It involves large computers and complicated math algorithms. It gives firms a competitive advantage," Michelle replied.

"How so?"

"It allows banks to make trades a fraction of a second faster than normal trades. If done in high volume, banks are able to generate a lot of revenue."

"Wait, so if I understand you correctly, Wall Street makes money off of trades because they have a bigger computer? Isn't that like, you know… stealing?"

"No. It's perfectly legal," replied Michelle.

"I know I'm just a poor kid from the projects, but please explain to me how Wall Street is able to generate money off other trades without the consent or knowledge of all parties and it's not illegal?" Barry started pacing as his voice went up an octave. This was happening too fast for him.

"We're getting off topic. Ana, proceed, please."

"Well, first I kind of borrowed some code from Wall Street."

"How did you borrow the code?" Barry used finger quotes to emphasize borrowed.

"Well, I set up a honey pot, because I didn't want to use our computer and—"

Michelle looked confused. "Honey pot?"

"A honey pot is a trap to catch hackers," Barry said. "It's old school. We did it in college. The theory is you expose your IP address or something and when someone tries to hack you, you actually hack them. But this still doesn't make sense. You still would not have enough horsepower to perform these types of trades. Right?"

Ana had always been an exceptionally bright child, but her IQ would need to be off the charts to have pulled this off. An IQ that undoubtedly had increased significantly the last few months or so.

"The IRS has plenty of horsepower. And with a lot of businesses filing their quarterly taxes over unsecured wireless connections, I was able to hitch a ride. After that it was fairly simple to install my software in the IRS's mainframe," Ana calmly explained, as she folded her arms.

Barry was resigned. He turned to Michelle and said, "You know we're going to jail, right? Please continue, Ana."

"OK. The software ran every day for a month and deposited the money into an offshore account in the Bahamas. After that I had enough money to design my own open source system using Ubuntu..."

For the next twenty minutes, Ana proudly explained in detail her office condo in New York, her software office in Bangalore, India, her fifteen thousand square-foot mansion in Florida, and other details about her business and life that her parents knew nothing about. There was a long silence after she finished.

"My head is hurting, but let me see if I can get this straight…" said Barry, rubbing his temples. "You accidently transferred two million dollars into your personal checking account instead of your business payroll account. And you have all this money because you 'borrowed' proprietary software from a Wall Street firm and had that software illegally installed on the IRS's mainframe computers. The IRS! And the IRS actually made daily deposits to an illegally created offshore account in the Bahamas. Those deposits were transferred to another illegally created account in Switzerland! A Switzerland account that is owned by an illegally created company that is in turn owned by a Chinese business man who doesn't exist!"

Ana stuck out her lower lip. "But Mandarin is the best vehicle for me to expand into emerging markets while maintaining a layer of obfuscation."

"What? I didn't understand a word you just said. Anyway… now this same illegally created business has a team of IT workers in Bangalore and support staff like HR, secretaries, legal and such, in New York?" Barry paused for a response.

"All that is accurate except for the legal part. I had Gram's firm do all the legal work. I figure, you know, someone else in the family should get paid, right?"

"You know what? I'm not surprised by that. Not even a little. Moving on… with profits from this illegal business—profits you didn't pay taxes on—you purchased a fifteen thousand square-foot mansion in

Florida with two swimming pools! Oh, and two hot tubs! Can't forget the hot tubs. And your mansion is owned by a trust that is controlled by an illegally created business in Brazil! And you probably speak Spanish, right?"

"Yeah, I do speak Spanish. But I learned Portuguese to set up everything in Brazil. You know, it's a common misconception about South America... oh, sorry." Ana went quiet as Barry glared at her for silence.

"And now the bank is probably reporting you, or rather me and your mother, to the Feds. This will probably trigger an investigation resulting in me and your mother going to jail!"

"Dad, daddy, father, no one really goes to jail for white collar malfeasance. Worst case scenario is I pay a fine. Trust me. You wouldn't believe the stuff banks get away with and the government doesn't even care."

"Great! That makes me feel me so much better! So a twelve-year-old child who is currently getting all C's—except for math of course. You are getting a D in math—has created the most complex international criminal apparatus I have ever heard of. Did I miss anything?" Barry sat down, then got back up while pacing and wiping his sweaty brow.

"But my math teacher doesn't even like me!"

"Seriously? Wow. I'm mean... I... I'm actually speechless." Barry took his glasses off, looked at them, and put them back on.

Michelle pointed toward the stairs. "Ana, go to your room. Me and your father will discuss this and let you know what we decide. Go. Now!"

After Ana had left the room, Michelle turned to Barry with a raised eyebrow.

He hated that look. "I know, I know. I'm on it."

Chapter 4

"Gwendolyn, we need to talk." In the week since Ana told her parents about her speed trading business, they were still undecided on what to do or even how to punish her. As promised, Ana shut down everything as it related to that specific business, but two days ago she'd discovered something extremely disturbing, and hadn't slept since.

"Band Geek, I'm talking to my friend!"

"Not right now! But later tonight; after the game."

"Yeah, OK. So anyway, Lizzy, isn't it cool that you made the team?" Ana was standing outside school with Gwen and Elizabeth while they waited for their perspective rides. It was the first week of October and the day was overcast and windy.

"I thought Ana was in orchestra? But yeah, it's cool making the team and all… But what's the deal with Eve and Amy? Don't they like each other?"

"They OK. It's just that they've been competing against each other for so long they don't know how to act. So, you know, they're still working things out."

"Actually, it is a bit more involved than that…" Ana was relieved to talk about anything. "Obviously, Eve still sees Amy as a competitor as opposed to a teammate. I believe the genesis of this friction is that Eve frames everything as a zero-sum game. Both having all honors classes and being constantly compared to each other by students and teachers just reinforces Eve's thought process. And Amy being über popular doesn't help."

"Hey, Super Dork, stop blaming Eve! It takes two to tango you know!"

"Agreed. But from what I observe, Amy has made friendly overtures to Eve. Plus, she has been telling everyone that she and Eve are going to be unstoppable this year."

Eve came up quietly behind Gwen. "What are you guys talking about?"

"Eve… we need to talk. It's important—" Ana started, before she was interrupted by Elizabeth.

"Hi, Eve! I love your dress!"

"This old thing?" Eve feigned surprise while she did a catwalk twirl, ending with her hand on her hip. "It's Rachel Roy. My aunt got it for me."

"Please, Lizzy, do not get this girl started on clothes!" Gwen laughed.

"Eve, seriously. Tonight we—" Ana started.

"Look, that new security guard is lurking again." Gwen noted, nodding at Mr. Jones.

"That handlebar mustache of his is ridiculous!" Elizabeth laughed, but Ana saw her glance at Gwen and Eve apprehensively from the corner of her eye.

Gwen was focused on Mr. Jones with an intensity that Ana only saw when she went at it with Eve. "I actually think the handlebar mustache is kind of cool. With his bald head and those guns, he looks like a strong man in a circus. But you know, every time I turn around he's right there. That's not cool with me. It makes me want to shave off

54

that mustache of his just to see how tough he is. Because I'm curious. I want to know how tough he really is…" Gwen stated, more to herself than anyone. She trailed off at the end so she was just above a whisper.

Ana noticed Elizabeth was staring at Gwen with an open mouth. "Gwen is just kidding. Don't pay her any mind."

"Of course I am! Hey Lizzy, want to come to the city with us and watch our cousins dominate in the state championship football game? Our grandmother should be here any minute." Gwen changed her demeanor and tone as if a switch had been flipped.

"Wow! A ride with your grandmother! I'll text my parents now! She is all my mom talks about! My mom wanted to be a lawyer too, but had to drop out of law school when she had me. That would be so cool to meet her. Is she really worth seven billion dollars?" Elizabeth asked while she texted.

"We do not discuss our grandmother's finances!" Eve spoke with an edge that stunned Elizabeth.

"Jeez, Princess! And Mom and Dad wonder why you don't have any friends."

"Elizabeth, Eve is correct. We do not speak of our grandmother's finances. But let me say this; that *Forbes* article is an estimate. An estimate that I would say is wildly inaccurate," Ana offered in a conciliatory tone. It was apparent that Elizabeth had not spent a lot of time around Eve. Eve was fiercely protective of their family and her sharp tongue and never-back-down attitude had put more than a few students in their place. Elizabeth had now discovered this the hard way.

"Super Dork, please stop talking."

55

"I am not a dork! I'm more of a nerd. Dorks do not have the social acumen to communicate effectively with people outside their primary area of interest," Ana replied, still doing her best to lighten the mood.

"You mean there are actual categories? I assumed the terms were synonymous?" Eve offered, in an overly friendly tone.

"No. There is quite a bit of difference between geeks, dorks, and nerds… with nerds being at the top of the food chain," Ana answered.

"Top of the food chain? You mean like being the tallest dwarf?" Gwen laughed.

The girls were still laughing and joking when Elizabeth's mom and dad pulled up in a sporty sedan. Elizabeth's mother got out, not looking pleased. Spotting her, Elizabeth stopped mid-sentence and bolted without saying goodbye. Her mother started yelling at her while the father stayed in the passenger seat. He looked like he was asleep.

"Well, I guess she won't be going to the game after all," Gwen deadpanned as they watched the car speed away.

"That was a bit peculiar," added Ana.

"Hey, if it's not too late when we get home tonight we should do a couple rounds of sparring. Plus, I have some new workout ideas."

"I respectfully decline your invitation to beat me up again. My entire body has been sore since we started your workout and sparring sessions," Gwen had been making her and Eve work out and spar every day after school. It was not Ana's idea of a good time. Extra padding or not, Gwen kicked like a mule and Eve was too fast to hit. Ana was nothing more than an itinerant punching bag.

"Plus, basketball is starting. I can't see us keeping up your workout schedule, while studying and practicing." Eve added.

"I'm carrying all honors classes too this year. And Ana never studies. Besides, we've been blessed with extraordinary gifts and I'm not going to let mine go to waste! I mean, we actually have super powers! Think about that!"

"So? You think that makes us heroes or something? We are not heroes, we are freaks, and this isn't a comic book. Besides, you've gotten too strong, now. Ana and I risk injury every time we spar with you, and I for one—"

"Wait!" shouted Ana, "I have to tell you guys something!" She was so tired she had almost forgotten.

"And...?" Eve looked critically at Ana with a raised eyebrow.

"Yeah, Super Dork, what is it?"

"When I was doing some research on possible new revenue streams, I stumbled upon some information from a defense firm. The firm just won a multi-billion dollar federal contract for providing security to essential personnel overseas—"

"So?" interrupted Gwen. "You hacked into another company. Big deal! Pirating games was how you got busted last time."

"Technically, I never pirated any games... Anyway, defense firms with a government contract are basically a license to print money. So—"

"Will you please get on with it!" shouted Gwen.

"Yeah, Ana, why is this so important?"

"I found a case study of a soldier who was injected with a virus. A virus that enhanced his strength and reflexes. Significantly."

"And this is important because…?" prodded Eve

"The soldier experienced accelerated cellular degradation. This resulted in headaches, nosebleeds, and bleeding from the ears. Sound familiar? The soldier eventually expired. The family was told he died overseas in combat and the body was never recovered."

"Um… OK, by expired do you mean he died?" Gwen whispered, leaning in.

Ana took a deep breath. "Yeah… uh yes, yes, that is what I meant or what it means."

"Maybe I'm being slow but I still don't see the connection with us?" Eve responded, as she lowered her voice and took a step closer to Gwen and Ana.

"The virus that was used to treat the soldier was stolen seventeen years ago." Ana's mouth went dry as she waited, knowing she had their full attention. "And the primary suspect was Dad's friend Dave."

"The scientist?"

"Physicist."

"Isn't a physicist a scientist, Super Dork!"

"Will you two cut it out? Go on, Ana."

"No charges were ever filed and the missing material was never discovered. Now, three years ago, Dave was experimenting with tabletop fusion (he is a nuclear physicist after all). Something inexplicable happened and there was an explosion."

Eve's eyes grew wide. "I remember that! It was in upstate New York. It was on the news for a month. Dave wasn't injured but there was something like five deaths. Mom and Dad were glued to the TV for a week."

"Right! But the process Dave used is not conducive to explosions. Anyway, a young boy was caught in the explosion and suffered massive blast injuries. It was assumed he wouldn't make it. But he made a miraculous recovery, during which time Dave became his legal guardian and checked him out of the hospital in the middle of the night. They've both been off the grid ever since."

"Off the grid?" queried Eve.

"Yes, no email, no credit card transactions, no bills. No electronic footprint at all."

"We need to tell Dad and Mom right away, and maybe even Grams." Eve spoke quietly. "Right? Right?"

"Eve, honestly I don't think they can help."

"So that's it! We just expire! No! No way!"

"Eve, calm down. I have a solution. I'll skip over all the medical terminology but I can acquire the materials to synthesize an antidote."

"Well, Super Dork, if you can do it, can't a doctor do it? How come we just don't go to a doctor? Why are we even talking about this?"

"Gwen, trust me when I say we do not want our condition becoming public. David is off the grid for a reason. So that means a doctor is out. Also, to acquire everything I need is going to require us engaging in some illegal activity."

"Can't you just hire someone to grab the stuff and make it? I mean you are superrich right?"

"Yes, I am superrich and yes, I could hire someone. But it would take a while to screen qualified individuals. Remember we are speaking of two separate tasks and skill sets here. I can hire some mercs to do a smash and grab and some lab techs to mix everything. But contrary to what you see on TV, there are just not a lot of highly skilled criminals out there who can pull this off. And besides, the fewer individuals involved the fewer failure points and risks."

"Mercs? As in mercenaries? I don't even know who you are!" Gwen shouted, throwing her hands up.

"Ana, this doesn't sound right to me. If the doctor can't help us, how long will your plan take?" Eve folded her arms, then put her hands on her hips, then folded her arms again.

"It should be operational within two weeks."

"And why can't we tell Dad or Mom about this plan?"

"Gwen, we are underage, so if get caught doing something illegal the repercussions would be minor. Plus, we could play it off as one of your pranks. If Mom or Dad get caught or are implicated they could lose their jobs, go to jail, or worse. Second, the information I just told you could literally put their lives at risk."

"OK, OK. I get it! When do we start and what do you need me and Eve to do?"

Ana attempted to stop her voice from shaking. "The plan is already in place but you are going to need your bike, and someone needs to accidently put a large hole in the basement wall when we get home."

"Hmm, I guess I can get with this illegal stuff. But I'm bummed. The evil-corporation-super-soldier-experiment thing has been done to death. It'd be cool if this involved magic, or dragons, or even aliens." Gwen shrugged

"There is nothing cooler than science." Ana forced a smile.

"Whatever. And I can't believe there aren't any supersmart criminals we can outsource this to!" Gwen continued.

"There are plenty of supersmart criminals. But most of them work on Wall Street," Ana advised.

A honking horn startled the sisters. They watched as their grandmother's black town car rolled to a stop.

Ana prayed silently to herself as she headed toward the car. Her plan had too many uncontrolled elements to confidently forecast a definitive outcome. She, however, had managed to vet a crew to build her home lab. Doing most of her research in-house would allow Ana to increase her profit margin in some business ventures and more easily branch off into other areas of interest like avian DNA. As she dreamed about her potential fortunes, her forced smile was replaced with a real one. But only for a second. She had to be alive to enjoy any potential fortunes.

***

"Ms. Parker, what is that in your hand?" Mr. Little strolled up unnoticed behind Ana, Madhuri, and the Booger twins. Mr. Jones, the security guard, stood stoically at his side, massive arms folded over his barrel chest.

"Excuse me?" Ana whirled around to face him while attempting to close her locker.

Mr. Little grabbed the door. He snatched the bag with his other hand and pulled out an extravagantly wrapped bag. The unwrapped bag revealed an extra-large, dark chocolate bar and an assortment of premium novelty candies.

The Booger twins disappeared into the background—an impressive feat given their rotund size and disheveled appearance.

"Ms. Parker, please tell me you are not selling candy on school premises?" Mr. Little sneered. He placed the candy under his arm and retrieved a large roll of money from the bag.

Ana was embarrassed. She couldn't believe she'd let Stacey and Madhuri talk her into selling candy. The pocket money it generated was convenient; that she was being confronted by Mr. Little, however, crystalized the fact that the risk was not worth the reward.

Mr. Little finished counting the money and placed it back in the bag.

"$377, Ms. Parker? I certainly hope you didn't acquire all this by selling candy?"

Ana didn't respond.

"Well, Ms. Parker, I think I'll hold on to this until one of your parents contacts me. Or maybe I can discuss it with them next week at Parent Teachers Conference?"

"But that's my lunch money!"

"Like I said, Ms. Parker, I will discuss this next week with your parents. I know you come from a family of considerable means, but… $377 seems a bit much for lunch money."

"Is everything OK, Ana?" asked Ms. Henderson, the first year assistant librarian. Ms. Henderson's pale skin and stocky build was in stark contrast to Mr. Little's tan, thin frame.

"Hello, Ms. Henderson. Looking rather nice today. I must say, black does become you… But I'm afraid this is nothing that concerns you. I was simply confiscating some contraband from our little Ms. Parker here."

"Is that true, Ana?"

"I guess." Ana looked at her feet. She could feel the disdain that Mr. Little and Ms. Henderson had for each other; the intensity and heat emanating from them was palpable. Ana didn't want to do anything to exacerbate the situation.

"There you have it. Again, nothing to concern yourself with, Ms. Henderson. And please don't be late for class today, Ms. Parker. You know how I abhor tardiness," Mr. Little said over his shoulder as he sauntered off.

Mr. Jones looked menacingly at Ms. Henderson, before following Mr. Little.

Ms. Henderson glared after them. "Are you sure everything is OK? Would you like me to talk to Mr. Little or the principal?"

"No, I will be OK, really. But thanks anyway."

"OK, But please, please let me know if you change your mind," Ms. Henderson offered before leaving.

"Super Dork, did you not learn anything from watching *The Wire*? You always keep your product and money separate." Gwen lightly popped Ana in the back of the head. "And who did Ms. Henderson sleep with to get a job here, anyway? Worst librarian ever! Seriously. The library is a mess! Last week I asked her what's up with the Dewey Decimal System in this piece and she said rap is next to the alternative music section!" As usual, Gwen was surrounded by a bevy of students the majority of whom were basketball players, who laughed at her jokes.

Eve walked up and stood directly in front of Ana, shielding her from Gwen. "Is everything OK?"

Ana nodded and was relieved for the distraction. She hoped practicing for a couple of hours would allow her to recharge her batteries and provide a fresh perspective on the upcoming challenges.

The girls bumped into coach Hall on their way to the gym.

"Hope you girls are on your way to practice."

"Are you kidding, coach? We will beat you there!" Gwen laughed.

Gwen's incessant chatter and jokes were cathartic. Ana had a plethora of challenges to overcome in a very short time and Gwen was a welcome respite. Fortunately, she did not consider Mr. Little one of those challenges. She knew he had no plans to tell her parents about the candy or money. That would force him to give the money back, and he probably planned to use it on hair products.

***

"No! No! No! Run it again. Eve, on a 'give and go,' you actually have to give the ball up!" shouted Coach Hall as he ran his hands through his thinning blond hair. "No, Amy! No! When Eve gets the ball to you and cuts to the basket, give it back! Hence the term 'give and go'! You girls are killing me! Run it again!"

It was the second week of practice and Eve and Amy were giving him an ulcer. Eve was more irritable and on edge than usual. Her attitude and temper had the team walking on eggshells. Amy took offense to this and openly challenged Eve at every turn. The collateral damage of this tug-of-war was a tense group of players who didn't trust each other enough to run the simplest play.

Two plays later, Eve brought the ball up court. She looked off a wide open Amy, drove to the basket, and missed a contested layup.

Amy glared daggers at Eve on the way down the court.

Coach Hall thought he should stop this as he ran his fingers through his hair again. Temperatures were running high, the players were getting chippy, and with Eve in the mix anything could happen.

The next play Eve attempted to split a double team. Melissa stripped the ball and passed to a wide open Toni, who raced down court making an easy layup. *Why are these girls trying to destroy my life?* Coach asked himself.

Melissa's team cheered. Amy yelled, "Pass the ball!" and the gym went quiet. Eve and Amy were both fuming.

"Eve, have a seat! Melissa, take her spot. Gwen, take Melissa's spot. Rebecca, you're in. Let's go! Run it again!" coach Hall yelled.

He didn't know what to make of the Parker girls. Ana had the best jump shot he had ever seen: it was effortless. The way the ball rotated off her fingers was a thing of beauty. But Ana wouldn't even

65

pretend to play defense, and the next time she went into the paint to grab a rebound would be the first time. Gwen was his hardest worker and best on-ball defender. Despite her size she was also the second best rebounder next to Amy. But this year she practiced like she was scared of contact— something she'd taken pride in last year. And Eve was an enigma; he had never seen a girl with her ball control and ability stop and start on a dime. It was breathtaking. But she never followed instructions, dribbled too much, and refused to play within the offense.

Melissa had the ball stolen twice by Gwen in back-to-back plays. Both times, Gwen passed to Ana for wide-open three-pointers that hit nothing but net.

"Melissa, just stab me in the heart and get it over with! I'm serious: you're literally killing me! Eve, get back in there. Melissa, Gwen, switch teams. Rebecca, have a seat! Come on! Let's go!" coach Hall growled while he prowled the sideline.

Eve began passing the ball to everyone but Amy, which did not go unnoticed by Coach Hall.

"Eve! Eve! Amy is open!" yelled coach, on one particular play. Eve ignored him and passed to Elizabeth, who fumbled the ball out of bounds.

"Rebecca, run and get the nurse! Tell her these girls are killing me... Rebecca, where are you going? Get back here!"

"I'm open! I'm open! Pass the damn ball!" yelled Amy the next play down while loudly clapping her hands.

Eve passed the ball to Lucia, who backed Amber down in the post before Gwen stripped the ball away and passed cross-court to Ana for an easy layup.

"Come on!" yelled Amy back down the court, right before the ball bounced off her head.

"I thought you wanted the damn ball!" Eve yelled. They stared at each other. No one in the gym moved. They charged.

Gwen intercepted Eve, lifting her off her feet with a bear hug. Coach Hall realized that Gwen must have anticipated this and had been shadowing Eve. Amy was barely being restrained by Elizabeth, Lucia, and Toni. The girls shouted, screamed, and cursed at each other.

Coach Hall finally managed to blow his whistle. Everybody stopped. "That's it! Practice is over! Over! Hit the showers!" As everyone walked off the court, he grabbed Eve's arm.

Toni and Lucia continued to hold Amy's arms.

Eve and Amy glared at each other until Amy disappeared into the locker room. Eve then turned her attention to coach Hall.

"What is going on with you this year? Your attitude toward me, toward your teammates, has been downright disrespectful. And that was before today's shenanigans. Is there something I should know? Something you would like to tell me?"

Eve looked at the coach, unblinking, without saying a word.

"Eve, do you want to play basketball?"

Silence.

"I said, do you want to play basketball? Because if you do, and you want to play for me, you have to clean up your act."

67

Silence.

"Eve, you have as much talent as anyone I've ever coached—including Amy—but it doesn't matter, because talent alone won't get it done. Listen, Eve, I love you; you know this, and I think you're a great kid, but something is going on with you and I can't help unless you tell me what it is."

Silence.

"You know I played football and basketball against your uncles when I was in high school. They were at all times the most talented players on the court and the football field. How they didn't go D1 or pro I will never know. But they played selfless ball. They made good teams great. You understand what I am trying to say to you?"

Silence.

"I am going to have to start Melissa over you." Eve opened her mouth to say something, but the coach raised his hand to silence her. He had a lump in his throat and his voice was starting to get raspy.

"No, I've heard it all before. I've talked, begged, and pleaded with you but nothing works. And you know, Melissa is nowhere near the player you are, but the team plays better and harder when she is in there because she always puts team first. Something I seldom if ever see from you."

Silence.

"Good night, and when you go home tonight, really think about if you want to play basketball. And if the answer is yes, then come back tomorrow and show me."

Coach Hall shook his head as he watched Eve walk slowly to the locker room with her head down and shoulders slumped. The team's chances of winning a championship were slim to none without Eve's talent. He ran his hands through his hair one more time before heading to his office. The kids in this school drove him crazy. They had everything money could buy but the problem was they knew it. And their parents were worse. If he had a dollar every time an irate parent threatened him with "Do you know who I am?" he could retire early. Closing the door to his office, he slumped down in his chair. *This job really is killing me*, he thought.

***

"Hello, Mr. and Mrs. Parker. I'm Anastasia's math teacher." Mr. Little stood as Barry and Michelle entered the classroom.

He directed them to two chairs facing his desk.

Michelle eyed him warily. She had heard the rumors about Mr. Little but was attempting to reserve judgment.

"And how are we both doing today? I trust we are doing well?" Mr. Little began.

"We're fine, thanks." Michelle replied, fearing his grandiose manner confirmed the rumors.

"Excellent... And please know I am a huge fan of your mother, Mrs. Parker. You know I come from a family of lawyers myself? Yes, I know. But I feel teaching is my passion. Touching young lives. Molding young minds. You know, I believe it was St Thomas Aquinas who said, 'We are like children who stand in need of masters to enlighten us and direct us: and God has provided for this, by appointing his angels to be our teachers and guides.' Is that not inspiring? I find myself referring back to that quote quite often, every time I feel I've made a difference. It's what I live for."

"Interesting… But would it be OK if we discussed Ana now?"

"Yes, of course…Our little Anastasia is quite the 'jokester,' isn't she?"

"Jokester?"

"Ah, yes. Our little Ana—"

"I'm not quite sure what you mean by 'jokester', but if Ana is clowning around in class I would definitely like to know." Michelle answered, while leaning forward and staring intently at Mr. Little.

"Oh, well now, I don't mean 'jokester' *literally*. I just meant to say that Ana is a bit loquacious is she not?" Mr. Little backtracked, while adjusting his collar and glancing at his watch.

"So she is talkative now?" Michelle continued, with an edge to her voice.

"Well, Mrs. Parker, as you know, students like to talk and play around. I am just sharing—" Mr. Little offered, while sliding down in his chair a bit.

"Mr. Little, I don't mean to be short but I'm here to discuss Ana, my daughter, not the other students. I am particularly interested in discussing her last test in which she got all the right answers but received a D."

"Ah, yes, well, she did not show her work. And there are questions as to how she arrived at the right answers without showing her work."

"I see... So how much do you usually deduct for not showing your work?"

"Excuse me?"

"How much do you deduct per problem for not showing your work? Do you deduct ten points? Fifteen points? Twenty points? I would like to know how much the answers are worth and how much showing your work is worth. Are they weighed equally?"

"Well, Mrs. Parker, I mean, showing your work is a very important part of the test. If students don't show their work, it raises questions... I mean it's all very complicated."

"Mr. Little, both my husband and I have our undergrads in mathematics, so as complicated as it might be, please humor us."

"Well, then, you must understand that not showing your work raises questions as to fair play. When students choose not to show their work it puts educators in the uncomfortable position of making assumptions. Again, it raises questions of fair play, you see?" Mr. Little explained, shifting in his seat.

"Yes, Mr. Little, I see very well and I agree with you. Showing your work is critical in test taking, especially math. I am simply asking you for a quantitative metric. How much is showing your work worth and how do you quantify it?"

"Well, of course, every test is different—"

"Mr. Little, I am not speaking of every test. I am speaking specifically of the last graded test that Ana took. The one where she received a D? You remember Ana, right? My daughter? The child we

71

are here to discuss? The 'jokester'? The 'talkative one'? You do teach seventh grade math don't you, Mr. Little?"

"Well, of course I do. What exactly are you trying to insinuate?" Mr. Little replied, raising his voice and sitting up in his chair.

"Insinuate? You mean like calling Ana a 'jokester'? This insinuates that she is disruptive or some type of class clown. The same Ana whose personality every other teacher before you has said they would like to see more of. Or better yet, your casual reference to Ana as loquacious. This of course insinuates that she is talkative in class. Again, this is the same Ana whose previous teachers say she is too quiet and needs to participate more in class discussions. Also—"

"Got him! Yeah! It's on now! Oh, my bad... so basically, Ana is a talkative class clown who cheats. Did I miss anything?" Barry said, while putting his phone away.

"Who did you get, babe?"

"My starting running back broke his arm in a bar fight. I just picked up his backup off of waivers. My other running back has a bye this week."

"Isn't that the same running back who won you the championship last year?"

"Yeah. The kid is a beast. So what's the story? Are we finished here?"

Michelle stood to leave.

"Yes, we are finished here."

Mr. Little was every bit as handsome and clueless as she had heard. He had no idea that Ana's IQ was off the charts. But Ana had better be more careful because, as naive as Mr. Little was, he was not stupid.

Twenty minutes later, Michelle and Barry were sitting in front of Mrs. Adams, going over one of Gwen's math tests. This was the second math test that Mrs. Adams had gone over and her enthusiasm and energy were contagious.

"Now, Mr. and Mrs. Parker, if you look at this problem, you can actually see the wheels turning in Gwen's head! Isn't that amazing? Look at what she wrote here, and now look at her answer! Can you see it?" Mrs. Adams looked at both parents expectantly.

Michelle always enjoyed her visits with Mrs. Adams. She was the type of teacher Michelle wished she'd had when she was in school. Mrs. Adams loved nothing more than teaching and it showed in every conversation.

"Yes. Yes, Mrs. Adams. I do see it. I hadn't noticed that before. Thank you... But now tell me, how do you feel Gwen is doing? Is there anything we should know about? Has she been behaving OK? Has she been a distraction in any way?"

"Well, to be honest, I had reservations about having Gwen in my class, her reputation being what it is and all. And especially with what happened last year to poor Mr. Freedman. But I think she's doing fine. She struggles at times. I mean, it doesn't come as easy to her as it did to Eve. But she is a hard worker and wants to do well and I couldn't be happier with her performance and attitude. I just wish she wouldn't put so much pressure on herself."

"I see, I see. Do you think it might be better to take her out of the honors program?"

"Oh, heavens, no! She is capable of doing the work. I mean, she still might get a B! My biggest concern is, now that basketball has started, will she have the time needed to study?"

Michelle turned toward her husband, "Babe, care to add anything?"

"Yes, Mrs. Adams, I think our biggest concern is the stress we see from our child at night while she struggles with her homework. We want our children to excel but not to the point where... where it consumes them. Does that make sense?"

"Yes, yes it does. And I don't want to minimize your concerns, but this is honors math. It should be challenging. Yes, Gwen struggles, but if the worst case scenario is she gets a C, I don't think it's the end of the world."

"Mrs. Adams, I think my husband and I both agree with you... a C should not be the end of the world, but this is Gwen we're talking about. We have some concerns, some worries. I'm sorry, this is, uh, we..." As Michelle struggled to articulate her concerns, Mrs. Adams gently grabbed both her hands and looked her in the eyes.

"Mr. and Mrs. Parker, I understand. I know. But I think Gwen is more resilient than you give her credit for. If she does get a C it might affect her for a bit but trust me, nothing can keep that young lady down for long."

"You're right. I think we have a tendency to overthink… over worry, if you will. Thank you for your time. As always, it was a pleasure meeting with you." Michelle rose and embraced Mrs. Adams.

Ten minutes later, the Parkers entered the classroom of Ms. Grant. Ms. Grant taught ninth grade honors English and was the pride of the school. She was Ivy League–educated, a published author, and the teacher most parents bragged about when they casually dropped the name of the school. Michelle noticed Barry stand up straighter and she had to admit that, on top of Ms. Grant's accolades, she was also very attractive.

"The Parkers!" Ms. Grant hugged Michelle. As usual Ms. Grant was dressed in all black. Her black leather boots stopped just at her knees and right before they met her black knit skirt. Her long sleeve black turtleneck was just tight enough to tease her lithe frame. Michelle didn't know what she ate or did to stay in such fantastic shape but, if they had time, she was definitely going to ask at the end of the conference.

"Please have a seat." Ms. Grant motioned Barry and Michelle toward two chairs. "OK, let me see here… ah, here they are." She flipped through a folder and handed Barry and Michelle each a set of papers. Michelle leafed through the papers as she sat down. She was relieved that Ms. Grant was now in charge of honors program as opposed to Mr. Freeman who had an unfortunate accident last year and immediately resigned.

"These are some of Eve's writings I had submitted to some national competitions. With any luck, we will hear back before Christmas. Again, her writing is as strong as ever. But I have to ask…"

75

Ms. Grant paused as she adjusted her schoolmarm glasses and briefly scratched her tight bun of coiled black hair.

Michelle leaned forward, "Yes, Ms. Grant?"

"Well, it's just that Eve has always been a quiet, serious student. But when I had her in seventh grade she was… more engaging." Ms. Grant said carefully, as her pale skin blushed slightly.

"I see…" Michelle replied.

"Eve appears to have pulled back socially. She is still one of my brightest students, and her love of books is endearing, but she keeps to herself more than I would like, and she also seems to have lost a bit of her focus."

"Ms. Grant, we understand. All the girls have been dealing with external issues that might be wearing on them. Not to make excuses, of course."

"Mrs. Parker, I don't presume to understand the type of pressures your daughters face day in day out. It's just that if Eve regains her focus she has an excellent chance of being valedictorian this year."

"I understand. But when you say she's regressed socially, can you provide an example?" Barry asked.

"I didn't say regressed. Regressed is a bit strong. It's just that she doesn't participate in class discussions unless prodded. And she has been less… I guess you could say *patient* with other students when working in groups."

"I see. Well, we'll definitely discuss this with her," Barry offered.

"I just wish she would share a bit more. She has so much to offer, after all."

"I understand, Ms. Grant. And thank you for your concern. This has been a challenge for us as well. Also I have a couple of questions about some of her writings…"

Chapter 5

Eve was losing patience as she listened to Ana. She had little confidence that Ana could gather everything in place, and even less confidence they could pull it off even if she did.

"OK, guys, it's Saturday and I have everything in place. Gwen, it would be nice if you can get your bike back by then," Ana said, as the girls waited outside of school for their mother to pick them up.

"Child's play."

"All I know is this better work, Ana!" Eve growled.

"Princess, you need to chill and stop being a jerk to everybody. Super Dork has everything under control. Ain't that right, Super Dork?"

"Was I talking to you, Gwen? Mind your own business before I mind it for you!"

"See? That's exactly what I am talking about!"

Eve knew she had a problem controlling her emotions of late. But being demoted to second string the same week you find out you're dying would be a lot for anyone to handle.

"Gwen, why don't you just worry about yourself for a change? And Ana, you better be right about this!" Eve stepped toward Ana.

"Back off, Princess! Your temper tantrums and pity parties are risking everything! So chill!" Gwen replied, stepping in front of Ana and squaring off against Eve.

"I... I just want to get this over with, OK? I'm tired of thinking about it and worrying about it." Eve conceded, as she exhaled.

Ana stepped around Gwen and put her hand on Eve's shoulder as their mother pulled up.

"I am worried as well, Eve. But we have to work together. OK?"

"OK, OK. I'm good." She could do this. She had no other choice.

***

Saturday morning.

"Hey, Dad, would you like some more eggs?" Eve asked her father, who sat at the breakfast bar reading the paper and drinking coffee.

"Why yes, I would." Eve was so nervous she couldn't stand it. She focused on keeping her hand steady as she shoveled more eggs on her father's plate.

"Hey, Dad, can I refill your coffee?"

"Yes, you can, Gwen, but before you girls continue being so nice to me, you need to know you can't go to the park until this house is clean."

"Say what? This house is huge! It will take us all weekend! How come we can't get another cleaning lady?" Eggs fell out of Gwen's mouth when she spoke.

Barry looked at her and pushed his eggs away. "Because I think the cleaning agency actually filed a restraining order this time. We had three cleaning ladies quit in one year. That's a new record for us."

"Can we get Rosa back?"

"No, Eve, Rosa is never coming back here. She won't even return my phone calls."

"I thought Rosa liked us. Why won't she come back?"

79

"Well, Gwen, if I had to put a finger on it, I would say the tarantula in her purse was the final straw. But don't worry about Rosa. She's still being paid for the rest of the year. As is Diane."

"I have absolutely no idea how that spider got in her purse. But she's surprisingly quick for a woman her size. How come we're still paying Diane? That was nobody's fault."

"Gwen, I think a court of law would find fault with whomever booby-trapped their bedroom."

"I keep telling everyone it wasn't a booby trap. It was a snare, and it was meant for Ana. So, Dad, after we clean the house can I have a mansion in Florida like Ana?"

"No."

"Can I get a set of drums?"

"No."

"Geez! What are we, Amish now! Can I at least have my bike back? Please?"

"Sure, after the—is that my phone?"

Barry answered his buzzing phone after retrieving it from under the newspaper.

"Hey, Bob, what's up? Really? The entire system? Again? Yeah. OK, give me thirty minutes or so." He hung up. "Girls, I have to run. Tell sleeping beauty no allowance this week. She knows why. And Gwen, nice use of the Overton window, by the way, but do not leave this house without cleaning it."

Gwen and Eve gave each other blank stares as their father rushed upstairs, then back down, and out the house.

"Good morning, Mother. Would you like some coffee, eggs, fresh-squeezed orange juice, and toast?" Eve asked her mother seven minutes later.

"And we know you like your coffee like you like your men. Right, Mom?" Gwen added, winking at her mother while handing her a cup of coffee.

"That is inappropriate and not funny. Eve, can you bring me my phone, please? Thanks." Michelle sat down at the breakfast bar and sipped her coffee.

"Yes, this is Michelle Parker. I see. Are you sure? Everybody? Right now? Well, if I leave now, depending on traffic I could be there within forty-five minutes. Yes, Mr. Andrews. I'll see you there."

Eve's mouth dropped. This had Ana's name all over it.

"When Ana wakes up, tell her no allowance this week, and if any one of you ever puts another IOU in the church collection plate, I will have your behinds."

"Ana is a multi-millionaire. She has a mansion twice the size of this house, with two swimming pools and a hot tub. Punishing her by taking away her weekly allowance is probably not a very good deterrent. Just a thought."

"Eve, stay in a little girl's place. Now, you two give me a hug before I go."

Eight minutes after Michelle left, Ana came downstairs still half asleep. "Mom and Dad leave yet?"

"Yes. But they really have emergencies?" Eve probed.

"One of Dad's production systems is down. Hopefully this will be the impetus they need to migrate off their legacy systems. And Mom's meeting is mostly about acquisition chatter. Anyway, Gwen, it's important that you eat as much as possible before we leave."

Gwen put more bread in the toaster. "I like this breaking the law stuff!"

Thirty minutes later, Eve and Gwen were on their bikes ready to leave for the park. Ana came out carrying three backpacks. She looked into each one before handing them out, then pedaled away, saying, "Follow me."

Ana led them across the street to the park, which was packed with two soccer games and a group of high school boys playing basketball. They followed the bike path into the wooded area for a mile or so, before Ana veered off road. Three minutes later, they stopped at a secluded spot among the trees.

"We can change here."

"Hey, Super Dork, quick question… are we ever going to get a cleaning lady again?"

"I have not had time to properly vet any cleaning ladies. And I do not want anyone in our home without being vetted."

"That stinks."

The girls changed into clothes from their backpacks.

Gwen looked herself and her sisters up and down.

"Hey, I thought we were going to be soccer players?"

"And?" Ana replied.

Gwen popped Ana in the back of the head. "We are wearing rugby shirts, genius! Orange and black rugby shirts!"

"Stop hitting me!"

"Stop buying rugby shirts!"

"Gwen, stop! Ana, that's true; these are rugby shirts. Not soccer shirts like we agreed on."

"Should it matter?"

"Your lack of attention to detail for something so simple is starting to undermine my confidence in you."

"We're dead!" Gwen added.

"I'm sorry. I've had a lot on my plate and besides, I got a great deal on these."

Gwen took a threatening step toward Ana. "What? We are going to die but at least you got a great deal, right?"

"I saved 25 percent! And you should start being nice to me! You don't know how much work I did to set all this up!" Ana shouted defiantly, standing her ground and facing Gwen.

"Say what? 25 percent? Really? Well, why didn't you say so! Hell, yeah; you can kill me twice for saving 25 percent!"

"Chill, Gwen. Ana, how come your shirt, shorts, and shoes are all black?"

"Because I'm the goalie."

"But these are rugby shirts! Does rugby even have goalies?" Gwen protested.

"Ana, this is not cool. We look like your bridesmaids!" Eve complained.

"But—"

"We're dead!" Gwen added again.

"Whatever. Let's just do this." Eve said.

Two minutes later, the girls had on Beatles-style wigs, dentures, and tinted athletic glasses. Lastly, they donned green baseball caps and put on green sweaters and tan khakis over their rugby uniforms.

"OK. Now remember, try to keep your earpiece covered at all times. And do not under any circumstances talk to anyone. Period. I will do all the talking. Our primary method of communication will be our earpieces."

"OK with me. What's with all this stuff, anyway?" Gwen asked.

"The glasses, dentures, and wigs are lined with an extra-dense material that will distort any hi-tech facial recognition cameras or X-rays we might encounter. And please remember to wear your gloves at all times, and try not to touch anything."

"Does anyone have a mirror? I want to see what I look like."

"Sure." Ana handed Eve a small mirror.

"Oh my God! I can't even recognize myself. It's amazing!"

"Yeah, Eve, you look totally different. If I didn't know any better I couldn't tell it was you."

"But Gwen, you should see yourself." Eve handed the mirror to Gwen.

Gwen looked at herself in the mirror. "Super Dork, you are a genius!"

"Come on guys, let's go. The cab should be waiting for us." Ana donned her baseball cap and tucked her hair in.

Gwen looked around. "But what about our bikes?"

"Oh yeah." A few feet along the path, Ana stopped and lifted a translucent camouflage tarp that had been invisible a second ago. "Put them under here."

Gwen and Eve obliged. When Ana covered them with the tarp they disappeared, blending into the surroundings.

"Cool," Gwen noted.

"OK, let's test our earpieces. Eve, say something."

"Ana is a dork! Or is it nerd? I honestly can't remember."

"Got it. Now you, Gwen."

"She will always be a dork to me."

"Got it. Now see if you can hear me. Testing one, two, and three. Testing one, two, and three."

Eve nodded. "Yes, we can hear you loud and clear."

"OK, we have a nice walk, so let's get started. Gwen, I tried to factor in your metabolism and body weight, but for now take two dosages and we will see how it goes."

"Sure." Gwen said, taking two small, brown plastic bottles from Ana and quickly downing them.

A few minutes later, they were out on the other side of the park next to their school. They walked another block and turned into an alley behind a large grocery store. Their green sweaters, tan khakis, and green baseball caps matched what the clerks and cashiers were wearing. A taxi pulled up and they jumped in.

"Seventh Ave. Downtown, please." Ana spoke with a Hispanic accent.

85

"Yes, yes, of course. You have money, right?" The cab driver replied, with a Middle Eastern accent that was not consistent with his online profile, Ana noted.

"Yes, we have money," Ana answered, while looking at his smiling face in the rearview mirror. His large mustache dominated his boyish face and apparently frightened his bushy eyebrows, which looked like they were attempting to flee for cover in his mop of thick, curly hair.

"Yes, yes, of course. I hurry," the cab driver replied, pulling away.

"OK, this is good. Can you pull into the alley? Thanks. Can you meet us back here in twenty-five minutes exactly?" Ana still spoke with a heavy Spanish accent and tipped the cab driver generously.

"Yes, yes. Twenty-five minutes, I be here."

The cab pulled off. The girls quickly pulled off their pants, sweaters, and baseball caps and stuffed them into their backpacks. They emerged from the alley wearing their rugby uniforms and walked a block down to Mercy Hospital. They ran across the street.

"Gwen, how do you feel?"

"Not good. Not good at all, little sis."

"You consumed five bottles, which even for your body weight and metabolism, seems exceedingly high. We will have to revisit that at a later date... OK, synchronize your watch and meet me and Eve back here in twenty-two minutes. OK?"

"I got it, I got it. I just need to sit down," Gwen whispered, and then stumbled.

"No! Ana, get her other arm." Eve draped Gwen's arm around her shoulder. Ana grabbed the other arm and almost buckled under the weight. Together they struggled into the emergency room and managed to sit Gwen down in the crowded waiting area. Ana and Eve gave Gwen a fist bump before they slowly backed away and waited.

After five minutes Gwen started vomiting. The volume and velocity was incredible. She sprayed everything and everyone around her. People started screaming, shouting, and running as they attempted to escape Gwen's breakfast. The emergency room cleared of patients in seconds.

"This way!" Ana grabbed Eve's arm and led her down a hallway. Ana checked her surroundings as doctors, nurses, and janitors raced past them to the emergency room.

Ducking into a laundry room, they put scrubs on over their rugby shorts and shirts. Grabbing a chart hanging on the wall, Ana instructed Eve, "Do not look anyone in the eye and again, no speaking."

They bumped into an orderly as they exited the laundry room. Ana admonished him in Spanish, pointing demonstratively at the emergency room before walking off in a huff.

"What did you say to him? My Spanish is not that good."

"I asked him where he's been, and how come he's not cleaning the emergency room."

"But how did you know he spoke Spanish?"

"Whether he speaks Spanish or not is immaterial. The goal was confusion. If he does speak Spanish, great. Gwen's making a mess and he should clean the emergency room. If he doesn't, also great. As long as he doesn't tell anyone he caught two girls coming out of the laundry room, I don't care."

"Ana, you scare me." Eve smiled.

Ana smiled back. It was not easy to impress Eve, and Ana could not help but feel a little proud. "OK, we have thirteen minutes to get up seven flights, break into the medical storage facility, get what we need, and get back outside."

"OK, I got it, but wouldn't it be easier to take the elevator?"

"Yes, it would be; easier to get trapped, easier to get caught. Let's go." Ana noticed Eve looking at her sideways. Eve did not like taking orders from anyone, let alone her younger sister, but so far she had put her ego aside, for which Ana was thankful.

They climbed the seven flights without any encounters.

"Stay close behind me," Ana instructed, as they stepped out of the stairwell.

She grabbed an empty cart and handed the clipboard to Eve. As she made her way briskly down the hall, her confidence swelled. Things were going as planned. Ana walked with purpose while the doctors and nurses ignored them. A left and then an immediate right and they were almost there. Ana turned the final corner and stepped quickly back.

"Hey!"

"Shh!" Ana peeked around the corner. She watched a nurse leisurely exit the medicine room with a loaded cart. The nurse looked around casually before getting on the elevator.

When the elevator door closed, Ana started to move, but Eve grabbed her arm and pointed at the ceiling cameras on both ends of the hallway, "Ana, what about the cameras?"

"I took care of those at home. In their hurry to upgrade and leap into the twenty-first century with a hi-tech security system, they left a back door open."

"Good to know." Eve smiled, shaking her head.

"OK, I should only be a minute. Use your earpiece if someone comes."

When Ana reached the door she noticed the doorknob had been mangled. The metal was twisted, rendering the lock ineffective. She entered the room, scanning it while her heart started racing. On the wall was an empty cabinet, the door torn off its hinges. Ana held her breath as she frantically checked the cabinet over and over again. Nothing.

She exited the storage facility and walked past her sister. "We have to go."

"Did you get the stuff?"

"No. I think the nurse beat us to it—"

"The nurse? That doesn't make any sense."

"We'll discuss it later." Ana held a finger to her ear, "Ms. Black, mission failure. Repeat, mission failure. Rendezvous at designated area in three minutes. Repeat, rendezvous at designated area in three minutes."

Three minutes later, Ana and Eve were outside the hospital emergency room doors. Scrubs discarded, they were back in their rugby uniforms.

"The cab will be here in two minutes. I wonder what's taking Gwen so long." Ana looked at her watch and shifted her weight from one foot to the other.

Eve headed for the emergency room. "I'm going in after her."

Ana held one hand to her ear and followed Eve. "Ms. Black! Ms. Black, we are coming in!"

Before Ana got to the emergency doors she could smell Gwen's handiwork. The stench almost made her gag. Apprehensively, she followed Eve through the sliding doors. The room was empty of patients. Gwen's breakfast was all over the floor, the walls, and the ceiling. Ana estimated Gwen consumed close to twelve thousand calories on a daily basis. But the emergency room looked as if she'd expelled three times that amount. Gwen was surrounded by a throng of doctors, nurses, and security. She tapped her ear and nodded, indicating she'd heard everything.

She looked drained, almost pale. She was backed into a corner, keeping everyone at bay with a chair. No one in the room paid any attention to Ana and Eve. Ana took out a phone and began typing.

"What! You have a phone?"

"Ms. Pink, not now… I need you to … Oh, uh!" Alarms and sirens went off.

"That doesn't sound good!" Eve said, looking around.

"The security system! It's re-booting! If we're not on the other side of the glass doors in thirty-nine seconds, we'll be stuck inside for the next seven minutes. Oh, and the fire department and police are coming!"

"What?"

"I'm sorry, I fat fingered it!"

"Just count down for me!" Eve tapped her earpiece. "I got this!"

Ana nodded and watched as Eve positioned herself behind two doctors.

"Twenty-eight!" Ana shouted, while she watched the seconds on her watch tick down.

Eve held up a fist to catch Gwen's attention. Gwen looked up and nodded. Eve held up three fingers. Then two. Then one.

Eve and Gwen spun into action simultaneously.

"Twenty-two!"

Eve did two front snaps to the crotch area of the doctors from behind. They immediately dropped to their knees. She kicked a nurse in the back of her leg, just beneath her knee. The nurse dropped as well.

Gwen tossed the chair to the side while trying to run without falling in her vomit. She ducked under the arms of one security guard as he attempted to grab her. She came up with an uppercut that lifted him off his feet. He landed on his back, three feet away. Still struggling to run, she stiff-armed another security guard in the chest. He went flying. The lights blinked on and off when he hit the wall.

Ana watched all this while keeping track of the seconds ticking away. "Seventeen!"

The remaining doctors and nurses paused as Gwen raced past them.

"Thirteen!" There was no way to quantify it, but Ana thought she might actually have the coolest and toughest sisters in the world.

All three girls turned to leave, but two more security guards rushed in from outside and blocked their exit.

"Ms. Green, stay close behind me! Come on, Ms. Black! Man up! We need you!" Eve shouted, as she took off at full speed, heading directly for one of the security guards. Gwen followed, veering off to face the other guard.

Eve juked right, then executed a spin move on her left, leaving the first security guard grasping at air. She raced outside untouched.

The second security guard rushed forward to meet Gwen. They crashed into each other head first. Gwen high-stepped over him as he crumpled to the floor.

Ana slid through the legs of Eve's security guard as he turned to face her after missing Eve.

She was two steps behind Gwen as they rushed outside to join Eve.

"And one!" The sliding glass doors slammed shut as Ana looked at her watch.

As they ran down the hill, Gwen looked at Ana. "I can't believe you have a phone!"

"Not now! Stay in character!" replied Ana.

They dashed across the street and into the alley. They snatched their khakis and sweaters from their backpacks and put them on as fast as possible. The cab pulled up as they were putting on their baseball caps.

"Yes, yes, twenty-five minutes, I come back. You smell something, yes?"

Chapter 6

The following Monday, Eve was one of the first players dressed for practice. She shot free throws with Amy and Lucia as the other players trickled in. Gwen assisted Elizabeth with low post moves at the other end of the court, but Eve knew that Gwen (along with everyone else) was keeping an eye on her, and had been since her dustup with Amy.

The scrimmage portion began with Melissa as the starting point guard for the starters and Gwen opposite her for the second string. Eve waited patiently on the bench. The events over the weekend had made basketball less important than it once was.

Two back-to-back steals by Gwen and Coach Hall placed Melissa on the bench, while Gwen switched to the starters and Eve joined the second team. It was the first time Eve had been able to participate in a scrimmage in over a week, and she intended to take advantage of it. Gwen attempted to pressure Eve but got crossed over, as Eve drove past her for a layup. When the defense doubled Eve she passed to a rotating Ana for a three-pointer. When Gwen had the ball, Eve harassed her into a bad pass, two double dribbles, and a carry. Gwen slammed the ball in frustration.

"Gwen, Eve: switch!" Coach Hall shouted after the second unit took the lead in points.

There were grumblings among the other starters, which Eve pretended not to notice. The first play was more of the same, with Eve blowing past Gwen for a layup. The next play, Eve was doubled and she hit a rotating Amy for an easy jumper.

Over the next few days, Eve regained her starting position and she played with a tenacity and control impossible to miss. She established a rhythm with Amy, and they became unstoppable when running the open court.

It was the last Friday practice before the first game of the season. Eve and Amy were in the zone. Eve was aggressively pushing the ball up court but playing under control. Amy was making every jump shot and attacking the boards. On one play, Eve's crossover move left Melissa stumbling. She spun off Toni and tossed a lob pass to Amy for an alley-oop lay-in. Eve glanced at the bench and saw Coach Hall was doing his best not to smile before he blew his whistle to end the scrimmage.

"Good work, girls, good work. We need to build on this and carry it over into games! Now I still haven't made a decision on the starting five, but we have seven or eight girls that can start for any team in the city! All right, everyone—thirteen sprints from end to end and hit the showers. Great practice!"

The team raced to the wall and started running. Eve took the early lead, followed closely by Amy, Toni, Melissa, and Gwen; the rest of the team were bundled together, with Elizabeth and Ana bringing up the rear. As the best distance runner, Toni usually won, with Amy coming in second, and Eve third. But Eve was not losing anything today. Pushing herself, she fought to stay ahead of Toni and Amy.

On the last three laps, Amy pulled even with Eve; Toni was a few steps behind both of them. This was usually where Eve hit the wall. But not today. Chest pounding, lungs burning, she pulled ahead. As her lead increased, she heard Amy grunting and struggling behind her. She touched the wall first and collapsed in complete exhaustion. She was soon joined by Amy, followed by Toni. All three started laughing as they cheered on and high-fived the rest of the team as they finished.

"Hey, Eve, I'm having a birthday party this weekend and I'd like you to come," Amy said, while they changed in the locker room.

Lucia winked at Eve. "Yeah, Eve, please come! Besides, I know a certain someone who has been going on and on about you."

Eve was shocked but maintained her composure. "This weekend?"

"Yeah, it should be fun. And Tyler is DJ'ing, so we are talking epic!"

"Sure. I'll be happy to come," Eve managed, with as much restraint as she could muster.

"Great!" Amy turned and walked out the locker room.

Oh my God, I am going to Amy's party! Everyone in school knew about Amy's party. It was the must-go-to event of the year. And Tyler was DJ'ing! Ana had told her earlier this year that Tyler liked her, but Ana had probably got her information from Stacey. Stacy was a nice girl but Eve did not consider her reliable. Although Lucia did ride the train with Tyler and she was definitely hinting at something. Eve was overcome with emotion and expectation. Sunday was two days away, her hair was a mess, she had absolutely nothing to wear, and she had to get Amy a gift that would steal the show.

Sunday! Since Eve's hair no longer responded to a hot comb, her mother had been experimenting with natural styles, none of which Eve had been fond of. But last night Michelle had spent two hours setting her hair with twist. An hour before Eve was scheduled to leave, her mother undid the twist in the powder room next to the kitchen. Each strand of untwisted hair stood out individually.

Eve looked in the mirror and, for the first time in a long time, she really liked her hair. It was unique, strong, and beautiful—like her. She also loved the way her dress fit her body. She now felt lucky to be blessed with her mother's curves.

As Eve stepped out the powder room, Ana ran up to her and handed her a pink silk gift bag. "Hey, Eve, it came an hour ago but don't worry, I already wrapped it! And I love your hair!"

"Move it, Super Dork!" Gwen shouldered Ana to the side. "Hey, your hair actually does look nice! How about that? Oh, and here, take these. Trust me, you really need 'em!"

Gwen handed Eve a miniature box of Altoids.

"Thanks, guys." Eve laughed. The girls looked at each other for a few seconds, until Eve ended the silence by hugging her sisters. "Thanks again. Really."

"OK, OK, enough of this mushy stuff and please take one of them Altoids now! You're burning my nose hair!" Gwen laughed, disengaging and pulling Ana with her.

Michelle grabbed Eve and inspected her at arm's length. Eve knew that her mother never got invited to parties or dances when she was young. Her grandmother had sent her mother to the most prestigious and competitive private schools in the city, schools that her mother had struggled at, socially. Eve had deduced this not from what her mother said but from what she didn't say. Her mother never talked about her time at school or mentioned any friends, a silence that spoke emphatically about her school experience.

Eve's father came downstairs before she left. "Hey, who picked out that dress? It's kind of tight, isn't it?"

"I picked out the dress. And there's nothing wrong with it," Michelle replied.

"I'm just saying. Isn't it kind of cold out, though? Shouldn't she cover up? Its flu season, you know."

"Bye, Barry." Michelle laughed, as she ushered Eve toward the door.

Barry stopped Eve and gave her a gentle kiss on the forehead. "Try not to break anyone's heart, OK, sweetheart? Boys are kind of fragile."

"Barry, we have to go." Michelle was smiling.

A short drive later they were parked in front of Amy's house. The car was still running but Eve didn't move.

"Hon?"

"I… It's just…" Eve began, while looking at her hands.

"Dear, you will be fine. OK? Have a good time and tell Dr. Sullivan I said hello."

"I will. And… thanks for everything."

Michelle nodded and Eve exited the car.

Amy's mother opened the door of their brick colonial home; she was as tall and beautiful as Amy. Her short, blonde hair curved around her slender face and her bright blue eyes.

"Hello, Eve! So glad you could make it. I've been meaning to call your mother about carpooling to some of the downstate games this year. How is she doing?"

"Thanks, Dr. Sullivan. My mother is fine and she would be happy to hear from you."

Eve followed Dr. Sullivan through a house that was tastefully decorated with refurbished furniture. "Everyone is in the back yard." She gestured to glass doors on the far side of the kitchen. "I am going upstairs to check on Amy who—surprise, surprise—is still getting ready."

Eve stepped through the doors out onto a large wooden deck that was twenty yards from an oval-shaped swimming pool. A brick pathway led the way to the swimming pool and surrounded it. A large brick patio was to the right and was being used as the dancing area. Eve set her gift down on a table that was already overflowing with gifts. She then closed her eyes, said a silent prayer, and ventured forth to join the party. It was not as big as she'd imagined. No more than thirty people at best, most of whom she recognized.

Kang, who was on the dance floor breakdancing with some other kids, acknowledged Eve with a nod. She smiled at him. Eve and her sisters had joined Kang's parents' Tae Kwon Do school six years ago. A year after that, Kang convinced her and Gwen to join the summer track club he ran for. They had been close friends ever since.

Tyler was at the DJ booth yelling encouragement to various individuals on the dance floor. Their eyes met. Eve's heart skipped a beat. Tyler smiled, yelling in his microphone, "We got Eve in the house, y'all!" Everyone on the dance floor turned and waved at Eve in unison.

OK. Nothing embarrassing about that! Eve thought.

During a break in the music, Kang joined Eve and offered her some lemonade.

"Thanks," Eve took the paper cup from him.

"What the heck did you do to your hair? It's different, but cool."

Her hand automatically went to her hair, before she caught herself. "Thanks. My mom did it. She thought it would look cute on me. You really like it?" She forced her hand back in her lap and smoothed out her dress.

"Yes, you look really good. Oh, and I heard about you and your sisters' performance at my parents' school last month. Why did you guys stop coming? My uncle has been on me non-stop to get you back. Even my parents are asking about you guys. My uncle says it was the most incredible thing he's ever seen, and he won't stop bugging me about it."

"My parents said we already had too much on our plate with school, church, and basketball. And they want us to start spending more time with our great-grandmother." Eve thought that her statement was basically true, if not entirely honest.

Kang nodded. "Well, if anything changes you should think about the Junior Olympics. You have a lot of talent and would do great with your foot speed. I would be more than happy to train you and it would be great exposure for my parents' school. Think about it…"

"Thanks, I will. Are you competing again this year?" Eve was anxious to change the subject.

"Naw, I'm going to put competing in Tae Kwon Do on hold for now and focus on football."

"So you're not going to Korea to train next summer, then?"

"Naw, I mean I'm glad I went the last few years and all. I got to spend some time with my cousins and the training there is crazy. That was the real reason I won Nationals. But you know football is my thing. My parents aren't happy, but I agreed to help out more at the school and stuff. That's chilled them out for now. But my mom is acting like I'm going to forget I'm Korean or something."

Eve, who knew more than most about the pressures associated with family and legacy, nodded, saying, "Yeah, I understand that."

"Hey, do you know where Walt is going? You can't turn on the news without them talking about him."

"Gwen probably knows. I haven't talked to him lately. His dad says he's been working out like crazy. You know how intense he gets. But I talked to Antonio and Emmitt yesterday. Emmitt is bragging about winning a championship without him."

"Cool, cool. Good luck to Antonio and Emmitt about getting that championship without Walt, though."

Eve nodded while scanning the party. She noticed it was primarily made up of the football, volleyball, and basketball teams with academics sprinkled in from Amy's honor classes. The most noticeable omission was Big John. Big John played football and was friends with Kang and Tyler. Eve was relieved he wasn't present; she shared a gym class and lunch period with him and hated the way he leered at her and the other girls.

Eve and Kang sat in silence. Eve was appreciative of his presence. Since she didn't run track over the summer she didn't get a chance to hang out with Kang. She now realized how much she'd missed him. Not saying a word, Kang got up and returned with more lemonade for her. They were soon joined by a small group of people who dominated the conversation.

Ten minutes later, Amy entered the party to loud cheers and an introduction from Tyler. She was wearing a dress by the same designer and style as Eve's, except hers was emerald green. They each noticed and shook their heads, while laughing. *The girl does have style!* Eve thought.

Amy made the rounds while Lucia commenced to detailing to Kang how great last week's practice was. She emphasized the moves Eve put on everybody. "I'm serious, Kang, this could be our year!"

"Nice dress, Eve!" Amy laughed, as she joined them.

"Why, thank you, Amy. It's from one of my mother's favorite designers, Diane Von Furstenberg. But it seems you're already familiar with her," Eve replied, laughing too.

Kang waved his hand dismissively. "Enough of that girlie stuff… Hey, Amy, is what I've been hearing true? Your girl Eve is breakin' ankles at practice every day with a killa crossover?"

"Yeah, Kang. You should see her. That crossover move of hers is unstoppable and her spin move is crazy too."

"My cousin taught me that spin move. It took me all summer to get it. But Amy is by far the best player on the team."

Amy looked surprised at Eve's comment.

The music was still playing when Tyler came over. Eve looked and saw Donny was DJ'ing.

Amy stopped smiling and put her hands on her hips. "Tyler what's up? I know you are not letting Donny spin?"

"Chill, superstar, I got this. Donny is posing. I have all the tracks preselected."

"I hope you're right. The only reason my mother let me have this party is because I promised no dirty dancing or profanity in the music."

Tyler looked at all the girls and smiled with his big dimples, saying, "You suburban girls need to chill. I got this—"

"Listen, Tyler... I'm serious. I don't trust Donny and you're supposed to be DJ'ing. If that nut does something, you're responsible."

"Trust me, superstar, everything is under control." Tyler turned to Eve. His mouth was smiling but not his eyes. His eyes were probing, questioning. "Oh, my bad; or are you the superstar?"

"We are both superstars. And we're going all the way this year!" Eve announced, as she hugged Amy around the waist and Amy reciprocated. But Eve and Tyler were having a private conversation. Her eyes questioned his intent, his sincerity, his heart.

Tyler nodded and turned back toward Amy, ending their private conversation. "No doubt, no doubt. So y'all talking 'bout a championship this year, huh?"

All the girls shouted, "Yes!" and on cue, Donny started playing a rap song laced with profanity that brought cheers from the crowd. The music sparked a different response from Amy and Tyler, who both raced over to the DJ table.

Tyler snatched the headphones off Donny's head while shouldering past him to the laptop. He quickly changed the music to something more family friendly. Amy towered over Donny and was speaking to him rapidly. The scene looked like a parent reprimanding a petulant child. Donny appeared unperturbed. He attempted to explain his side but Amy wouldn't let him get a word in. After a minute of this, Donny left the DJ area and took a seat. He looked around, smiling like nothing had happened.

Eve laughed at this and started to relax. She opened up and enjoyed conversations with students she'd known most of her life but had never talked to. Intermittently, she stole glances at Tyler, and each time he looked away, smiling. An hour later, Amy's mother arrived with the cake. Everyone sang "Happy Birthday," except Tyler, who sang the last verse by himself. He amazed everyone. Amy successfully blew out the candles and her mother immediately started serving cake. Shamelessly, Tyler put two pieces of cake on his plate and commenced eating with his hands while everyone watched him.

He shrugged off the attention, saying, "This is how we do it in the city!"

Amy laughed, set her fork down, and started eating with her hands as well. Most of the party mimicked this and soon everyone was eating cake, licking their fingers, and laughing unabashedly. Although Eve declined any cake, she couldn't remember the last time she'd had so much fun.

Once everyone was finished, Amy opened her gifts. She got mostly clothes, gift cards, and books. One of the last gifts she opened was Eve's. It was a leather-bound first edition copy of *To Kill a Mockingbird.*

"No! No! No way!" Amy shouted, before looking around and composing herself. "How did you know?"

"Oh my God!" added Lucia, who almost knocked Donny down to get a better look at the book.

"I remember you and Lucia talking about your favorite books last year. Since it was one of my favorites, too, it was easy to remember," Eve answered.

"You remember that? Aren't Scout and Atticus the best?"

Laughing, Eve said, "Yes. Yes they are."

Her brow knotted, Amy's mother pulled Eve to the side, "Eve, this book must be very expensive..."

"Don't worry, Dr. Sullivan. My sister says she got it for a great price."

"Well, I guess..." Amy's mother folded her arms but didn't sound convinced.

Kang sidled up next to Eve and Amy. "So, superstars, I bet me and Tyler can spot y'all seven points and still win in a game of two on two!"

"No, no, I don't think so." Amy grinned, shaking her head. "I've seen both of you shoot and we should be spotting *you* guys the points."

Kang laughed and motioned Tyler over from the DJ booth.

"So, dawg, these girls here think they got what it takes. They think they got enough game to beat us! The Original Dream Team in a game of ball! I'm just sayin…" Kang turned to Tyler, shrugged his shoulders, and feigned astonishment.

"What? Are we talking about…? I mean, I know we are not talking about… I mean, I know we cannot be talking about a… a… challenge!" Tyler shouted. The boys stood behind Tyler and Kang, laughing loudly and egging them on.

Not to be outdone, the girls stood behind Amy and Eve shouting taunts at Tyler and Kang.

Amy winked at Eve, saying confidently so all could hear, "Yeah, we can take 'em." To which the girls cheered loudly and the boys booed.

Tyler and Kang posed in identical comically fake martial arts stances, and screamed, "Challenge!" in unison, sparking another round of cheering and laughing from the boys.

Eve felt herself getting caught up in the moment. Laughing, she said, "Bring it on!" to more cheers from the girls.

Kang and Tyler were now standing in a B-boy pose, with arms crossed and chins up in the air. "Monday after practice! And don't be scared!" Tyler shouted.

"Oooh," parroted the boys.

Eve and Amy both laughed, saying "OK," at which point Amy's mother walked over, saying, "Eve, your mother is here."

Eve had been having such a good time she hadn't noticed how late it was.

Tyler took out his phone, saying, "Wait! We have to exchange numbers. You know, just so we can call you if you chicken out."

Looking sideways at Tyler, Amy smiled. "Whatever, Tyler, you're not slick."

"Yeah, mate!" said Donny, who had been standing nearby. Donny was a small, wiry kid from Australia. He had only been in the States one year, but was known by everyone and somehow managed to be at every party, invited or not.

Everyone stopped to look at Donny before continuing with their conversation.

"Sorry guys, I, uh, lost my phone. Thanks for the invite, Amy. I had a great time." Eve hugged Amy and a couple of the other girls before turning to leave.

Tyler grabbed her hand lightly. "I better walk you to the door. This is a big house. I would hate for you to get lost or something happen to you before your butt whipping on Monday."

"For real, though!" said Donny, for some reason. He started to walk out with them before being grabbed by Kang.

With the exception of a few whispers, the crowd went silent as they left together.

Eve turned her head to the side and feigned a cough while she slipped an Altoid into her mouth.

They reached the front door without saying a word.

Turning to face Eve, Tyler cleared his throat. "I'm glad you came, Eve. You're kind of cool."

"Is that supposed to be kind of a compliment?" Eve replied, placing a hand on her hip while the Altoid danced on her taste buds.

"Well, yeah, I mean, you know everyone says you're mean and stuck-up and stuff, but you're nothing like that," Tyler replied, looking down and rubbing the back of his neck.

"Well, I guess I'm happy that your unconfirmed secondhand talk about me proved to be unfounded," replied Eve, with mock indignation.

"Ouch! I guess what I meant to say is… well, you're smart, and funny, and cool, and… and… well, you look, I mean, you are beautiful. You're beautiful, Eve..."

The Altoid melted away. Eve grabbed his hand; it felt cold to her touch. The butterflies in her stomach tried to break out. Slowing her breathing she looked up, smiled, and whispered, "Thanks. Thanks, Tyler… you're kind of easy on the eyes yourself."

Laughing lightly, Tyler gently grabbed her other hand. Tyler's eyes asked questions. Questions about her. Questions about them. Eve's eyes acquiesced. He smiled.

An eternity passed before Eve finally stood on her toes and gave him a kiss on the cheek. She didn't look back as she rushed out the door to her mother's waiting car. Her feet didn't touch the ground. She was still feeling euphoric and dizzy when she went to bed that night. Her last thoughts were Tyler's words, "You're beautiful, Eve."

Chapter 7

"Oh! My! God! You have to tell me everything! Everything! I heard Tyler and Eve made out in the middle of Amy's party, right in front of everyone! Everyone!" Stacy and everyone else in school were all abuzz about Amy's party over the weekend. A couple of teachers told Ana to tell Eve good luck for the much-talked-about two on two basketball game. Stacey as usual wanted to know everything. But Stacey as usual would not let anyone get a word in.

"Oh, I wish I could stay after school today! I miss everything! Ana, you have to tape the game! You have to! Amy and Eve are going to crush Kang and Tyler! Right? *Right?* Oh, Kang and Tyler are so cute! Hey, did you guys hear about that aborigine rugby team that caused a riot at the hospital? They stole all the drugs and stuff! It's all over the news! My mother says any girl who plays rugby is crazy anyway. My dad says it had to be an inside job."

Madhuri looked at Ana and they both rolled their eyes.

Unexpectedly, Gwen reached over Ana and grabbed her sandwich.

"Hey, Gwen, stop it!"

"Chill, Band Geek! I'm just making sure it's not poison! You can never be too careful." Gwen laughed as she shoved Ana's sandwich in her mouth. She held one finger up for silence while she chewed. Finished, she gave the Vulcan hand sign saying, "Live long and prosper, nerds!" and walked away with Rebecca and Dana in tow.

"Wow! Ana, your sisters are so awesome! Does she know we're in orchestra and not band? Oh, and Eve is so beautiful! Did you see her hair? Awesome! And I wish I could have seen Gwen beat up on Bobby. Nobody likes Bobby! Nobody! I bet no one ever makes fun of Gwen! Hey, Ana, me, and Maddy are losing money hand over fist. You have to come back. We can't make the cute little bags like you! Right, Maddy? Right? So now, some of our most loyal customers are going to our competitors! You believe that? Even the Booger twins! Tell her, Maddy!"

Stacey was right about one thing. The hospital incident had been all over the news. Ana had intentionally chosen a cab driver whose background would lend one to believe that he would not be too enthusiastic about talking to the police. She had also tipped generously enough to let him know she paid for more than a cab ride. So far she had guessed right—the cab driver had not made any attempt to contact the police, at least not by phone or email. But the material still needed to be acquired, and hospitals and pharmaceutical companies were the only sure bets. And pharmaceutical companies were too risky.

"So, Ana, are you coming back? Please? Please?" Stacey persisted.

"Can't do it, Stacey. My parents would kill me if I got busted again." Selling candy was the furthest thing from Ana's mind. She had to figure out how to break into a pharmaceutical company.

***

As usual, Eve was sitting by herself at lunch, reading. Her focus was interrupted by thoughts of the weekend. The thoughts left her smiling.

109

Those happy thoughts were in turn interrupted by memories of the hospital fiasco the weekend before. Eve stopped smiling. The conflicting emotions fought each other for dominance. She attempted to re-focus on her book, but she just saw words that she kept re-reading over and over. And people kept interrupting her to say hello and wish her luck. This was unusual; students usually left Eve alone. She, however, was cognizant of what they said about her: she was called the poor little rich girl with no friends. That didn't bother her; she enjoyed reading alone. She had experienced over a thousand adventures, romances, and mysteries all over lunch. The other students wasted their time gossiping about people they didn't like to people that didn't like them.

"Hey, Eve. Care to join us for lunch?" Kang asked while approaching her table. Amy and Lucia were with him.

Kang had asked Eve to join him at lunch almost every week since school started. And every week she respectfully declined. Eve knew Kang was just being a concerned friend. But Kang sat at the alpha table. The joke in the cafeteria was that the alpha table was RSVP only. This was funny because it was mostly true. The best athletes and most popular girls sat at the alpha table; average did not make the cut. Most of the alphas consisted of two and three sport stars and cheerleaders. The only exception was Donny.

Eve had continually turned Kang down because she didn't feel comfortable around Big John and Amy. She knew Big John told everyone that her grandmother was rich because she was a shakedown artist. Up until last week, Eve had been on an uneasy footing with Amy.

But Amy was no longer an issue and Eve realized she was giving Big John more power over her then he warranted.

Eve stood up, as everyone stopped eating and talking. "Sure, Kang."

And here we go! Eve thought, following Kang, Amy, and Lucia.

Her eyes met Tyler's right away. His eyes were unsure; they had questions.

"So, anyway, it was hilarious! We were in tears. It went just like… and Big John, correct me if I'm wrong," Kang said, grabbing an apple from Tyler's tray and slapping Tyler's hand when he attempted to snatch his apple back.

"No, dawg! You wrong!" Tyler jumped up, laughing. "Give me back my apple!"

"This apple?" Kang took a bite, while laughing. "What you scared of Tyler? What you scared of?"

"You know what? Go ahead! I don't even care!" Tyler sat down, folded his arms, and tried not to smile.

"Anyway, we were playing Lincoln and getting crushed. I mean these cats were huge! Even their cheerleaders looked like they were on steroids. And coach was like, 'We just need one touchdown, gentlemen. One touchdown and we can hold our heads up high.'"

The football players at the table interrupted Kang with laughter and shouting.

Eve glanced around. Everyone in the cafeteria was watching Kang and the other alphas with approbation. The alphas were oblivious to this; Kang and his friends either enjoyed the attention or were ignorant of it, and Eve didn't know which was worse.

Kang continued, laughing, "So it's like fourth down, right, with eight seconds in the game. And Lincoln probably set the district record for sacks that game. I mean, they started sacking me during warm-ups and didn't stop until we got back on the bus. So I'm like, coach is crazy. I'm going to take a knee so we can get out of here. But Tyler comes back to the huddle and he's like 'Yo, run the bootleg joint and hit me on a fly!'"

Eve was not accustomed to this. She heard the laughter but she couldn't join in. She didn't feel happy—she felt confused and out of place. Outside of Kang, Amy, and Lucia, these people were not her friends. Except maybe Tyler.

"So, my man Tyler is amped in the huddle. He gets the rest of us amped and Big John is like 'Tyler is right! We can do this!' So I'm starting to feel it now. I'm like 'Yeah, let's do this!' We break the huddle and everybody is fired up. I mean the score is 42 to 0 and we think we got a chance!"

Kang pretended the apple was a football. "So we hike the ball, and I'm scrambling with the rock."

Kang dodged imaginary defenders. Everyone in the cafeteria was enthralled by his performance, even the teachers. *Tyler, Amy, and Kang practically ran the school*, thought Eve. They could do no wrong.

"Yo, I could have been on SportsCenter! I'm doing spin moves. Cats are flying past me. Then I see my boy Tyler beat double coverage and head for the end zone. So I put everything I had on this pass. The ball traveled like forty yards on a rope! Best pass I have ever thrown! Tyler turns around and the ball is on him. And I'm like, *yeah, touchdown*! But Tyler acts all surprised like, 'Hey, someone is throwing balls at me!'"

The table roared with laughter.

Were she and Tyler friends? Were they more than friends?

"Wait! Wait! It was like this!" Kang used the half-eaten apple to pantomime the football hitting his hand, then bouncing off his head, then bouncing off his other hand, and then bouncing off what would have been his face mask and falling to the ground. The laughter got louder. Tyler jumped up, shouting, "That's not how it happened! That's not how it happened!" He playfully pushed Kang to the side when Kang attempted to console him.

Eve slipped away unnoticed. She didn't think she was ready for the attention that the alpha table attracted. But she couldn't get Tyler out of her mind. Maybe it wouldn't hurt to give the alpha table another shot; but not today. When the final bell rang she headed to practice with a sense of relief.

She was joined by Gwen, Ana, Toni, and a few other girls. The students in the hallway made a clear path for them, with some shouting, "Go, Eve! Good luck!"

Gwen put her arm around Eve. "No autographs, please! No autographs! Talk to our people and we will try to schedule an interview after the game!"

During practice the shots were not falling for anyone. Coach Hall was acting more frustrated than usual. Practice was running long.

113

Everyone was tired and ready to go home. After a fumbled pass by Amy, Coach Hall shouted, "Again! We have our first game of the season in three days and we cannot run one simple play? Do it again!"

The play started with Eve at the top of the key motioning for everybody to get in position. Two seconds later, Amy got open. Eve tried to hit her with a bounce pass. Amy fumbled the ill-timed pass and the defense retrieved it. "Again! Run it again!" the coach yelled. "And do it right this time!"

Eve started the play again. She dribbled to the top of the key, mentally and physically exhausted. Gwen's workouts, stress, homework, and basketball practice had finally caught up with her. She motioned for the players to get in position. Amy started running, trailed closely by Melissa who was on defense. After Amy reached her spot on the court Gwen went in motion. Amy turned quickly, heading in the opposite direction. Melissa pursued Amy and ran into Gwen's pick. Amy caught Eve's pass in rhythm. With no defender within seven feet she hit a wide-open jumper.

"Finally!" the coach shouted "Now, run it again!"

But everyone was looking at Melissa, who was still on the ground. She'd run into Gwen headfirst and bounced off like she'd hit a brick wall. Her breathing was steady, but she was unconscious.

"Get back! Get back!" The coach shouted, running to Melissa. Students had started entering the gymnasium in anticipation for the battle of the sexes. The boys' basketball team had finished practice ten minutes ago and most of them were already there. Gwen was kneeling next to the coach, not saying a word. Ana and Eve stood directly behind her, each with a hand on her shoulder.

Melissa opened her eyes.

"Melissa? Melissa don't move. You were out for a minute and you might have a concussion," the coach said quietly.

Melissa smiled and said, "Does that mean practice is over?"

Her response gave everyone permission to begin talking and smiling. Everyone except the Parker sisters.

"All right, girls, that's it. Everyone go home. I'll update everyone about Melissa later tonight. Go! Stop standing around and go!" The coach exhaled and ran his hand through his hair. Eve and Ana attempted to console Gwen, but she pulled away as they headed for the locker room.

Amy, Kang, and Tyler were talking together. They turned to watch Eve as she followed Gwen. Eve shook her head. They all nodded.

When the girls got outside, there were a few students talking in small groups. Their father was waiting outside his car. He had a defeated look on his face that Eve could see him attempting to mask as Gwen ran to him. Their father knelt down and held his daughter as she cried. Eve and Ana walked slowly to the car. Eve watched as Gwen's shoulders shook and her back vibrated with the force of her emotion. Nothing was said. Nothing needed to be said. Like Tae Kwon Do before it, basketball was now over for the Parker Sisters.

Chapter 8

"OK, girls, after you finish eating breakfast you have a doctor's appointment," Barry announced Saturday morning with Michelle at his side. The Melissa incident had forced Barry's hand. He and Michelle could no longer wait for help from David that might never come.

"With a doctor?"

"Yes, Gwen, with a doctor. Your father and I think it would be best."

"Is that wise?"

"What do you mean, Ana? Your mother and I have no idea what is going on. We're worried. We need more information to help us decide what to do."

"Hello, Mr. and Mrs. Parker! So nice to see you and the girls again! Let me get your paperwork, so you can get started and I'll notify the doctor that you are here."

"Thanks, Helene. And it's good to see you too. How are the grandkids?" The doctor's office was located in the same strip mall as the Tae Kwon Do school. It was a small, no frills office and Helene sat behind a counter that separated the examination rooms from the waiting area.

"Oh, Mr. Parker, those boys are a handful! I'm afraid my daughter bit off more than she could chew with those two!" Helene replied, with a hearty laugh. Sitting behind the raised counter she was dressed casually, with old-fashioned reading glasses. Gravity and her girth conspired against her as she struggled to stand and hand Barry a clipboard. She patted her silver perm and settled back down in the chair. Her pale cheeks were flushed and Barry wondered if she would be able to rise again to go home.

Barry settled in his seat and filled out the required information. As they waited for the doctor, he started having second thoughts. *Might be better to keep it in the family and let Michelle's cousin take a look at them*, he thought. He was two seconds from leaving when the doctor walked in.

"Barry, Michelle, how is everything? Barry, I couldn't tell from your message how urgent the situation was with the girls, but I'm happy to take a look. Why don't you all follow me to the back?"

Dr. Weaver led the family to an open examination room.

"Please give me a minute. I'm flying solo today. Some kids went wilding in Nancy's neighborhood last night. Left her and a few neighbors with four flat tires. Kids today, I tell you. It was simpler back when we were growing up. Right, Barry? Anyway I'll be with you shortly."

He returned a few minutes later.

"OK. Eve, let's start with you. I'll just take your temperature right quick…Whoa! That can't be right. Let me try it again…Eve, it says here your temperature is 103 degrees. Are you feeling OK?"

"Yes, I feel fine."

"OK. Hmmm… let me try this…" The doctor tried a different thermometer in her ear. "Huh, 104? But that's just not—"

"Jim… please continue with the examination."

"But Barry, a temperature that high is dangerous. I can't—"

117

"That's what my message was about, Jim. Something has happened to the girls, and we are trying to figure it out, but as of now we consider an elevated temperature normal for Eve."

"OK. Well… I mean, I have no idea what we are dealing with. I tell you what: let me move some things around and I'll set up an appointment for the girls at my downtown office where I can take all the blood work, perform a more thorough examination, and be discreet."

"How soon can you do this?"

"Well, let me think… it's going to be at least a week. I'll have Helene call you with the details."

"Thanks, Jim."

"Not a problem. Now let's finish up here…"

Dr. Weaver continued his examination of Eve, and the other two things of note were an exceptionally developed musculature and extremely fast reflexes.

"OK, Gwenny! You're next! Up on the scale!"

A pause.

"Wait, Gwen. Step down again. The scale is off."

"No, Jim, the scale is fine."

"Alrighty then… that's 221 pounds." The doctor shook his head while writing. "Gwen… I'm… I've never seen a musculature like yours. It looks normal at first glance but is incredibly dense and developed at closer examination. I… I am totally befuddled. We definitely have to set up an appointment downtown. This is absolutely amazing." Dr. Weaver's breathing had been increasingly rapidly while constantly licked his lips but his enthusiasm when examining Gwen still caught Barry by surprise. "How strong did you say she is, Barry?"

"She's able to bench press five hundred pounds thirteen times, as of last week."

"Amazing. Absolutely amazing. OK, Ana, you're next." He performed the tests. "Hmmm, everything checks out OK for you... except your heart rate, which is twenty beats a minute. That's lower than marathon runners."

"She can also stay underwater for thirty-three minutes and make her heart stop beating for two minutes!" Gwen offered.

"Well, I would have to see that, because the mind does not control the autonomic nervous system, no matter what you have heard about monks and such."

"OK." Ana laid down, closed her eyes, and slowed her breathing. "Tell me when to start."

The doctor set the timer on his watch and placed a stethoscope on Ana's heart. "Go!"

No one moved. Three minutes later, Ana opened her eyes and gasped for air, startling everyone. She immediately started sweating and rubbing her chest. She looked exhausted. The doctor kept his stethoscope on her heart until her breathing and heart rate returned to normal.

"You feeling OK now, Ana? That was remarkable! I am just... wait, we'll talk later. Barry, Michelle, can I see you outside for a minute, please?"

The doctor closed the door behind them.

"I know you want answers here, but I am afraid I can't provide them at this point. I have absolutely no idea what I'm dealing with. Your daughters' conditions defy science. Unfortunately, until I conduct a more thorough examination, including blood workup, I don't have much to offer. Are both of you OK with this so far?" Jim asked, while he continuously licked his lips.

"Yes, Jim. I guess my biggest concern outside of finding out about their health and well-being is protecting the anonymity of my family. So, can all this be done with that in mind?" Barry was confident that if Jim were a cartoon he would have dollar signs in his eyes. He was practically drooling at the opportunity to examine the girls.

"Of course. The university has more equipment and Nancy will be the only person assisting me, and all the blood workup and labs will be done there. I understand your concerns and I will be as discreet as possible. Now, before we go back in, is there anything else you would like to share with me?"

"No, Jim. Not at this time."

"Very well, but keep in mind I cannot provide an accurate diagnosis without all known data and information being made available to me."

"Understood."

***

"Barry, you are a grown man. In a house full of women, I might add, so you might as well get accustomed to purchasing these items. Now hurry home and please don't be late for dinner." Michelle hung up.

Great! Barry thought, as he cruised the aisles in Costco. The fact that Michelle could have just as easily up picked up these items on her way home perturbed him, but he had to pick his battles so he was keeping his powder dry. The secrecy surrounding his daughters was starting to eat at him and he struggled with not telling his brothers. But maybe Mr. Brown was an option. He would know how to handle this. But how would that conversation start? "Hey, Nino! I ever tell you about the time I got drunk in Vegas, let my boy from college operate on me, inadvertently destroying the lives of my unborn daughters?" Barry shook his head and smiled grimly. He had no good options.

Scanning the aisles, Barry stopped smiling and thought about what his neighbors had told him a couple months back. They said two separate crews of at least seven people had worked on patching his basement wall and they'd filled two dump trucks with dirt. Barry was not a carpenter, but he wasn't a fool either. The girls were involved in this somehow, someway, and he needed to figure out how. And it had been over a week and still no word from Dr. Weaver. Barry's head started spinning. So many things were happening at once it was almost impossible to sort the important from the trivial.

He refocused on his task at hand as he casually glanced around the store. Not recognizing anyone, he took off down the aisle, thinking, "In and out."

"Mr. Parker? Mr. Parker?" a female voice called.

Looking around, Barry saw a short, plump lady hurrying toward him. Trailing her was a tall, distinguished-looking man in a dark suit that looked like it cost more than Barry's entire wardrobe.

121

"Hi, Mr. Parker. My name is Holly, Holly Newman. My daughter goes to school with your girls," stated Mrs. Newman, cheerfully.

"Oh, hello, Mrs. Newman."

She grabbed Barry's hand with both of hers and gave him an energetic handshake that almost pulled his shoulder out of its socket. After she released him, Barry stepped strategically in front of his cart to shield his items. Holly laughed at his attempt at subterfuge.

"Oh, please, Mr. Parker... with as many women as you have in your house, you should be used to buying those!"

Why does everyone keep saying that? Barry thought.

"As I was saying, my daughter Elizabeth is good friends with Gwen."

Barry moved past his initial embarrassment. "Elizabeth? Oh, yeah, Gwen talks about Elizabeth all the time. She says she's excellent in math and that she made the basketball team."

"Yes, we thought we'd let her try basketball this year, but it seems a bit much with piano and her studies and all..." Mrs. Newman responded, while glancing at the tall, sullen man next to her. "And let me introduce you to my husband, Michael."

Barry extended his hand. Michael appeared conflicted for a second before accepting it.

"I'm a big fan of your mother-in-law. Huge! You know I'm a paralegal myself and my husband practices law." Mrs. Newman put her husband's business card in Barry's hand.

Mr. Newman cleared his throat and stiffly walked away.

"Oh, I'd better run. And I would absolutely love to meet your wife. Let's all get together soon." Mrs. Newman energetically shook Barry's hand again before following her husband.

The lingering smell of alcohol disturbed Barry. Shrugging his shoulders, he pushed the cart full of feminine products toward the checkout and blamed himself for not letting his wife's call go to voicemail.

***

"Jupiter!" Ana blurted out during dinner with her family in the formal dining room. An idea popped into her head that she had to get out. An idea that, thankfully, did not have anything to do with hospitals, rogue nurses, or breaking into pharmaceutical buildings.

Gwen, who was sitting next to Ana, swiped a piece of chicken from Ana's plate, threw it in her mouth and, while chewing, asked, "What is wrong with you, Super Dork?"

"Is everything OK, dear?"

"Great, Mother! I'll be right back!" Ana dashed from the large mahogany dinner table and soon returned with a box of matches.

Barry set down his fork. "Uh, Ana, what are those for?"

Ana looked at her father at one end of the oval table and then at her mother at the other end. "I finally figured out how Eve moved so fast."

"But you already said it's an enhanced fight or flight response or something?"

"No, Mother, what I actually said was her fight or flight response has increased exponentially. But what I figured out is the fuel that makes that movement possible."

Gwen looked around the table.

"Really? Well, what is it?"

"First, let me try something... Eve, give me your hand." Ana struck a match and reached for Eve's hand who was sitting opposite her.

"And that would be a... *no!*"

"Trust me." Ana blew out the match and struck another.

Slowly, Eve extended her hand.

"OK, palm down, fingers open. Relax, Eve, relax." Ana slowly moved the flame closer to Eve's hand. "Only move it once the heat becomes unbearable, OK?"

"OK."

Aside from Miles Davis playing in the background, the house was completely quiet. The flame was now in direct contact with Eve's skin. She looked confused but did not move her hand.

"OK, let me try a couple of matches." Ana struck two matches and the flame touched Eve's skin again. Same results.

"Hey, that is actually pretty cool," Gwen said, after Ana blew out the matches.

Barry pushed his plate away and sat back. "OK, Ana, will you please enlighten the rest of us as to what this proves?"

"Look at Eve's plate."

Eve's food was untouched.

"What is this, a test? Are we being graded? Will you get on with it, Super Dork!"

"OK. Eve's movements are fueled by amplified electrical charges that are derived from CO_2 via carbon fixation (think plants and photosynthesis) and utilized by her central nervous system. To dissipate this excess electricity, her body speeds ups. That's the only way it can burn it off. Carbon fixation also converts CO_2 into proteins and sugars that Eve uses as her primary fuel source."

Taking off his glasses, Barry closed his eyes, pinched the bridge of his nose, and quizzed Ana, "So the speed is Eve's way of burning off excessive electricity? And you got all that from matches?"

"No. It was a bunch of things, really... Eve's hair does not respond to a hot comb, her internal body temperature is hotter than her external body temperature, she doesn't consume enough calories to fuel said strenuous activity... Voila!" Ana finished smugly.

"So basically, Eve moves fast to discharge excess electricity? Electricity that is a byproduct of her central nervous system and is triggered by her fight or flight response?" a confused Barry asked.

"Exactly."

"Ugh! This is giving me a headache!" Gwen rubbed her temples. "But why don't the matches burn her?"

"I hypothesize that the heat generated by the electricity is equivalent to that of a lightning bolt. In short, if her body was not able to adapt to these extreme temperatures they would kill her."

The family went silent.

"Oh, and she has a boyfriend," Ana added for good measure.

Chapter 9

"But he refused to come at the game!" Tyler laughed, "He was just padding his stats! It was ridiculous!"

"What do you mean, mate?" Donny asked.

"We were killing these cats. It was like 33 to 9 at half time. And all their points come from free throws!"

Kang smiled, folded, his arms, stretched out his legs and proudly announced, "But I still had a triple double!"

"But it's not legit! You was playing against scrubs! Coach was so mad he couldn't talk! He kept trying to send James in to replace him, and Kang kept waving him off. I thought coach was going to call security!" Tyler exclaimed, to laughter from the table.

As everyone got up to leave, Eve tugged Tyler's sleeve. Tyler dapped up Kang and the other guys. "Check you cats at practice," He told them, before leaving with Eve.

Eve and Tyler walked down the hall holding hands, "So what do you think about Langston Hughes now?"

"My bad. You were right. That cat is deep. How did you know I'd like him?"

"You have an intelligence and passion about you that reminds me of his poetry."

"You…you really think so?"

"Tyler, you're amazing. And don't let anyone tell you different."

"Eve, you are amazing. I have never met anyone like you. You got a brotha reading poetry. My boyz going to think I'm going soft." Tyler laughed.

"Would that be bad?"

"No, Eve. No, it wouldn't."

"Hey, can you have dinner with me and my family?"

"Sure, but it's going to be tight until after basketball season."

"I know. It's just that my crazy sisters were talking about you the other night and now my mom and dad want to meet you. Ana lied and said you were my boyfriend."

"So, I'm not your boyfriend then?"

"Well, I mean... I don't know... It's just that my parents are so strict. I guess…"

"No, its cool, Eve. I understand. I get it. But I probably won't be able to make dinner until after basketball season."

"But we usually eat late, so you can come over after practice."

"Eve, Eve, it's not that simple. After practice I have about an hour to catch the last express train to the city. If I eat at your house I'll miss that train."

"How about the weekend?"

"The weekends are no good. Mom's finally got that second job. I'll be watching my sister. Plus I told Harold I'll help him get his car running this weekend."

"Who is Harold?"

"Harold. The janitor. We used to ride the train together sometime. He lost his job here last week. I promised to help him with his car so he can look for jobs off the train line."

"The janitor at this school?"

"Yeah, Eve. We talked about him. Cool, older cat. He comes to all of my games."

"OK, I remember that. Well, how about catching a later train?"

"You know how far I live? And if I miss that express train it would take me over three hours to get home on a regular train."

"Tyler, this shouldn't be that hard. Is something else going on?"

"Eve look… I would love to sit down and have dinner with your family and meet your mom and dad and stuff, but it's just not possible the next few weeks. OK?"

"Can you just skip practice or something? My parents are expecting you this week."

"Are you serious? What, you think this school has some type of urban outreach program or something? If I don't play ball, I don't go here. Period. Let me get kicked off the team for missing practice and see how fast they discover my real address. And this school wouldn't miss a beat. Besides, you know I catch the train with Lucia."

People started to gather around as Eve and Tyler continued to raise their voices. Eve knew she should stop. She knew this was not the time or place, but she had to say one more thing and then she would let it go. "Well, why do you have to catch the train with Lucia anyway? Why are you making this so difficult? I don't think you are being fair about this, Tyler."

"Fair? Fair! Man, you suburban girls kill me! You want fair? I spend two hours every morning on two trains just to get here! And another two to get home! I do this so I can go to a school without metal detectors, police dogs or the fear of being shot for looking at someone the wrong way! And my older brother and Lucia's older brother were best friends—"

"But I—"

"No, Eve, check it! We talking about being fair, right? Right! Now, my brother is dead and Lucia's is paralyzed. She has no one else to walk her home at night! And trust me on this: you don't want be walking at night in our neighborhood, alone or not. So to be fair, I can't make it to dinner with your perfect little family anytime soon!" Tyler's voice was cracking. He abruptly turned around walked in the other direction. Eve was left alone, embarrassed, and ashamed.

****

"Ms. Parker? The board please?" Mr. Little pointed to an equation on the board. Ana was getting tired of Mr. Little's attempts to engage her. He woke her from her naps for no reason. He made constant references to her grandmother and her grandmother's wealth. And on top of all that, he was not a very good teacher.

"Ms. Parker," Mr. Little repeated, as he pointed to an equation on the board again. "What would be the first step in solving this problem?"

"One could take multiple approaches as a first step in solving this equation. But the answer is eighty-nine," Ana said, just as the bell rang.

Everyone quickly gathered up their materials. Mr. Little steamed. "Ms. Parker? Ms. Parker! Please do me the favor of staying after class."

"I'd love to, Mr. Little, but unfortunately I have a prior engagement. Let's put something on the calendar for early next week." Ana spoke over her shoulder as she walked out of class.

At her locker she heard the squeak of the mop bucket. Turning around she saw him: the new janitor. He was tall. Taller even than Tyler. But it was his head that gave her pause. It was enormous. It looked out of place on his thin frame. His hands were also abnormally large, with huge protruding knuckles. Looking at his facial structure, Ana deduced he was a victim of genetic manipulation or steroids, or both. His massive jawline could be an indicator of an overbalance of testosterone.

They are getting ready to make a move, she thought. The janitor had only been at the school for a month, but for the last week she always noticed him near her locker after the last bell. Ana made it a point to be at her locker the same time every day, while instructing her sisters to change their schedule as much as possible. They were definitely going to try something in the school and Ana wanted to increase the probability they chose her. She just wished they would hurry up. The Parker sisters were running out of time.

***

"So, again, sir—what makes you think it is foul play?" The police officer stood stoically next to his partner in the middle of the Parkers' sitting room.

"I didn't say it was foul play. I said it was suspicious," Barry responded, eyeing the clean-shaven, hulking police officers.

"So let me see if I understand you correctly. You take your daughters in for a routine check-up. The doctor schedules a follow-up in a week or so, but he doesn't call you back. You then discover that he was killed in a car accident. And by chance all his office computers contracted a virus, making any data recovery impossible. Is that accurate?"

"Yes," Barry answered, but something about these officers was off-putting. Outside of being enormous, their uniforms were brand new—even their shoes. Also, they weren't taking any notes and their mannerisms reminded him of Michelle's brothers, who were military. Michelle had ushered the girls out of the room when the police arrived, and Barry was glad that she had.

"Mr. Parker, we checked. Dr. Weaver was killed in an accident. The driver of a large rig fell asleep and crossed over the median, taking out three civilians including your doctor. We are still looking into this computer virus but it looks pretty routine, and it was not limited to your doctor's computers. Now I'm not trying to minimize your concerns, but I'm just not seeing foul play or a grand conspiracy here."

"But you have to admit it sounds awful suspicious. And like I said before, I think it might be all related to a college friend of mine."

"Well, Mr. Parker, I have nothing to go on here. Nothing to investigate."

"Officer, I know, I know. All this sounds strange and maybe it's just me, but something doesn't feel right about this."

"Mr. Parker, the case is closed—unless you can provide any new information. What about this David Hamilton character from college? What more can you tell us about him? When was the last time you talked to him?"

Barry noticed a perceptible change in the tone of the officers. A chill went down his spine. He had never mentioned David's name. Either the officer had slipped or he'd intentionally mentioned it as a not-so-subtle warning. "You know, officer, I can't remember. But I'm sure it will come back to me. I have your card so I'll be in touch."

"Are you sure, Mr. Parker? We would hate to leave without putting all your fears at rest."

"No. No, officer, we will be OK."

"OK, Mr. Parker. But let me leave you with this… you say Doctor Weaver was killed after examining your daughters. Correct?"

"Well, officer, I might have—"

"Correct, Mr. Parker?"

"Yes, officer."

"Well, Mr. Parker, if your story has any merit—and mind you, I'm not saying it does—but if your story does have any merit, it seems to me it would be extremely risky to let anyone else examine your daughters. Do you understand me, Mr. Parker?" There was absolutely nothing subtle about that.

"Yes, officer, I do. I think you better leave now." Barry was in a daze. The enormity of what his family was up against stunned him. If the police were involved, there was literally no place they could go and practically no one they could turn to. The officers tipped their hats and left. Locking the door, Barry shuddered involuntarily. A knot had formed in the pit of his stomach.

"Barry?" Michelle was wringing her hands as she entered the room.

"Babe, it's a good thing we didn't have your cousin look at the girls." He attempted to smile but failed miserably. Time was up; it was time to push the panic button.

Chapter 10

Gwen was sitting in math class when Elizabeth entered.

"Hey, Elizabeth, haven't talked to you in a while. How was your Christmas?"

"Oh, it was OK; I got a bunch of clothes, a new laptop, and a new phone." Elizabeth held out her phone for Gwen to see. "So what did your family do for Christmas?"

"We spent Christmas with my Grams in the city." Truth was, Gwen and her sisters had been on perpetual lockdown since the police visit. It was a week before they were allowed to leave the house and go to school. Ana had to convince their parents that following a normal schedule offered more protection and safety than staying home. Their parents acquiesced only after Ana acquired encrypted cell phones. Only their parents had the numbers, so their parents actually managed to take away the fun of having a cell phone.

"Your grandmother's? Really? At her penthouse? I've seen pictures in magazines and on TV. Does she really own the top floor? Does she really have an elevator that only she uses?"

"She owns the entire building. The top floor is the living quarters. Everybody that visits uses the elevator, unless they want to walk up fifty flights of stairs."

"Still, it has to be awesome!"

"Yeah, it's pretty cool. Hey, Lizzy, we still have some cake and ice cream from my birthday. Want to come over?"

"Will your cousin Antonio be there?"

"No."

"Aww. Hey, has Walter decided what school he's going to?"

"Walter will announce his choice when he's ready."

"Now, his father Benjamin and uh, Antonio's father Baldwin are your father's brothers right?"

"Geez, you ask a lot of questions, Lizzy! Yes, they are my father's brothers. My father is the youngest of four boys. Uncle Benjamin is the oldest. That's Walter's and Emmitt's dad. Then Uncle Baldwin, who is the father of Antonio and Antoinette. Then Uncle Brian, and my dad."

"Sorry about all the questions, it's just that your entire family is so cool and interesting. It's exciting! But I thought you couldn't have people over for your birthday?"

"What? Who told you that?"

"Everybody! They said last year at your birthday party, you and Melissa mummified somebody with duct tape and tied him to a basketball pole. They said the ambulance, police, and fire department showed up and everything. They said the paramedics had to use surgeon scissors to get the tape off and some skin and hair came off with it."

"What! That is totally not true!"

"So all that stuff about the paramedics, police, fire department, skin and stuff never really happened?"

"Oh, well yeah, that happened. But we got busted before we tied him to the basketball pole. You can't believe everything you hear, Lizzy. So you want to come over or not?"

"I'm sorry, I can't. I'm supposed to go straight home after school. I have to practice."

"We have a piano! And you can play piano and eat cake! Fun, right? Awesome, right?"

"I'm not sure. I could really get in trouble. My parents were not thrilled about the basketball thing."

"Geez, Elizabeth! I thought you said your mom liked us? It'll be cool. Trust me." Gwen was determined to have someone over for cake and ice cream and Melissa had soccer practice, the Booger twins had drama club, Toni and Dana were going shopping, and Rebecca was too annoying.

"I can't, I just…can't—"

"It's just cake! No one can get in trouble for eating cake! It's like, un-American!"

"OK, OK, but your mother has to take me home right after, OK?"

"Not a problem. I already told her you're coming, so I'm sure she'll be happy to drive you home."

"Hi, Mrs. Parker," Elizabeth said, as she climbed into the car after Gwen.

Michelle's eyes grew wide. "Oh, hello, Elizabeth."

"Hey, Mom, Lizzy needs a ride home, but I told her it would be OK if we stopped and got cake and ice cream first. Is that cool?"

Elizabeth's mouth opened and shut. Michelle's eyes narrowed as she looked at Gwen through the rearview mirror, before saying, "Sure, not a problem. I'll be happy to take you home, Elizabeth."

A few minutes of uncomfortable silence passed, until Michelle said, "I understand you are quite the pianist, Elizabeth."

"I'm OK."

"Oh, I'm sure you're just being modest! I grew up playing the piano myself and still enjoy sitting down every now and then, when I have some free time. Do you have a favorite classical piece?"

Elizabeth brightened. "I guess I like all of the pieces from Maurice Ravel's *Le tombeau de Couperin...*"

"Really? Do you know the Toccata? That is one of my favorites."

"Yeah. That's one of my favorites, too."

Michelle pulled into the garage and smiled at Elizabeth in the rearview mirror. "How wonderful! Would you mind playing it for us?"

"Sure."

"Great! Girls, show Michelle to the music room, while I take my files to the office."

"Can we have cake first?"

"No, Gwen, but you can have cake after."

When Michelle met the girls in the music room, Elizabeth was at their black baby grand piano playing a medley of the hottest pop tunes. Eve and Gwen were laughing while practicing the latest dance moves, as Ana watched, also laughing.

"OK, girls, settle down!" Michelle instructed. Her daughters complied and Elizabeth began to play Michelle's favorite classical piece. The next five minutes, Elizabeth wowed Michelle and the girls with some of the most beautiful music ever played on their piano. When she finished they gave her an ovation.

"Your parents must be very proud of you!"

"Now can we have cake?"

"Yes, Gwen, now you can have cake. Help yourselves. I'll be in my office, so please keep it down to a dull roar."

Elizabeth was on her second piece of cake when the doorbell rang. She turned white. "Where's my phone!"

"You left it on the piano." Gwen said, jumping up to the answer the door.

Standing outside was Mrs. Newman. She looked over her shoulder and then into the house.

"Is Elizabeth here?"

"Yeah, come on in, Mrs. Newman." Gwen smacked icing off her lips.

Something was wrong with Mrs. Newman. Gwen noticed Mr. Newman get out of the passenger seat and stride toward the house.

Mrs. Newman shouted to her husband. "It's OK. It's OK! I'm getting her now."

Michelle was now standing next to Gwen. They both moved out of the way to let Mrs. Newman in the house, and then closed ranks to block the door. "Hello. Can I help you?"

"Yes, yes, you can help me. I'm here for Lizzy," Mr. Newman snapped, with bloodshot eyes and his expensive suit in disarray.

Gwen could smell the alcohol emanating from him.

"Well, Elizabeth is having cake and ice cream right now. I'll be happy to bring her home as soon as she is finished."

"Listen… I do not need your permission to see my own daughter. Lizzy, Holly, let's go!"

"No! I'm sorry, but I cannot let this child leave with you in your current state."

"Listen, Mizz Parker, just because you're Josephine's daughter, that doesn't give you the right to walk over people and do whatever you want!"

"Mr. Newman, sir, please just calm down. Would you like to come in for coffee?"

"No, I don't want any coffee! And my wife and daughter better be out here in one minute or else!"

Michelle was breathing heavily but did not respond.

Without warning, Mr. Newman reached past Michelle. He grabbed Mrs. Newman by the arm, snatching her outside. Michelle grabbed Mrs. Newman's other arm. She tried to pull her back in. "Call the police! Call the police!" Michelle yelled.

Gwen was frozen. This could not be happening.

Mr. Newman won the tug of war. Using Mrs. Newman, he pulled Michelle closer to him and slapped her down.

This jolted Gwen into action.

She jumped over her mother and pushed Mr. Newman away; he flew back head over heels, landing several feet away.

Eve joined Gwen, breathing hard. They stood protectively in front of their mother. With Ana's help, Michelle struggled to get up. Gwen didn't see Mrs. Newman or Elizabeth.

Mr. Newman slowly got to his feet. He spit blood. He walked forward with a controlled intensity. Gwen and Eve did not move. Mr. Newman stood directly in front of the girls and raised his arm to slap Gwen. Gwen felt a rush of air on her right side; something flashed past her. Eve was now on her left, taking deep breaths. Mr. Newman doubled over, holding his stomach. The vision of her mother getting slapped overcame Gwen. Before she could stop herself, Mr. Newman was flying through the air from her uppercut. He hit the ground like a sack of potatoes and did not move.

Gwen turned to her mother.

"Oh my God, I'm sorry. I am so sorry!" Mrs. Newman was saying, over and over again, while hugging Michelle.

"It's OK. It's OK, Mrs. Newman. I'm fine. Really." Michelle pushed Mrs. Newman away gently.

Gwen saw the discoloration on her mother's cheek and her now-red eye starting to tear. Anger welled up inside her. She set out for the prone Mr. Newman once more.

"No, Gwen! No! Stop!" her Mother shouted, and grabbed Gwen's arm.

"Gwen, stop! Stop! It's not worth it!" Ana added, grabbing Gwen's other arm.

Gwen could feel her mother and sister but they offered little resistance. She heard their pleas but their voices did not register. She dragged them along effortlessly.

Police cars pulled up, blaring sirens, which snapped Gwen out of it.

Four policemen jumped out. One assisted Mr. Newman. Michelle, her left eye swollen, rushed to meet the other officers.

The youngest-looking officer began taking notes from Michelle, but was interrupted by a recovering Mr. Newman.

"I was attacked! I was attacked! Arrest them! Arrest them now! What are you doing! Arrest them!" he shouted at the police officers.

"Sir, can you take it easy?" an officer told Mr. Newman.

"I told you I was attacked! I want those Parker girls arrested now! Now!"

"OK, sir, that's enough. You need to… hey!"

Mr. Newman lunged at Gwen.

Gwen was ready, but a blur temporarily blocked her vision. She blinked, heard a crunch, and then Eve was next to her with hands on her knees, trying to breathe. A second later, Mr. Newman grabbed his nose, which started spewing blood. The officers stopped and looked at each other. Gwen did not stop. She kicked Mr. Newman in the ribs, directly under his raised arms. Mr. Newman went flying like a rag doll. He slammed into the maple tree in the Parkers' front yard, slid roughly down its bark, coming to rest in a sitting position with his back against the trunk.

Michelle grabbed Gwen and Eve. The police looked confused. Mr. Newman was gasping and struggling to breathe. One hand was holding his ribs, while the other constantly wiped away the blood that flowed from his fractured nose. Two officers finally went to his aid.

The ambulance arrived as the neighbors came out to watch. The four officers retreated to the sidewalk where they talked in hush tones as the paramedics looked after Mr. Newman. One of the four raised his voice—"No!"—and was quickly hushed by the other three. He whispered something, pointing emphatically at Gwen and Eve, which appeared to agitate his colleagues. The one taking notes leaned forward and whispered something in his ear. The conversation stopped. The first cop looked at the other three in disbelief before stomping away to sit in a police car by himself.

Michelle herded her daughters toward the house. A paramedic interrupted her to inspect her face.

Gwen was shaking. She didn't know if it was because she was mad, nervous, scared, or all three. Ana and Eve put their arms around her when Mr. Newman started shouting.

"Holly! Holly! It's not my fault! It's not my fault!" Mr. Newman struggled to say, while he was strapped into a gurney. His speech was garbled and barely intelligible. Mrs. Newman turned away. Elizabeth didn't. She stared with tears in her eyes, not flinching. Gwen pulled away from Ana and Eve and grabbed Elizabeth's hand, squeezing it.

"Elizabeth. Elizabeth, honey, you know I didn't mean it. You know I love you and your mother. Please. I ... I'm sorry."

Gwen had never heard a man sound so pitiful. So desperate.

Elizabeth stared at him silently, tears streaming down her cheeks.

"Elizabeth! I'm sorry!"

One of the officers handcuffed him to the gurney as they loaded him into the back of the ambulance.

"I'm so sorry!" Mr. Newman shouted one last time, while sobbing.

Gwen's cheeks were wet. She'd just wanted to have cake and ice cream with a friend; she'd been through so much, surely she was owed that.

The policemen finally left. Michelle and Mrs. Newman supported each other as they ushered the girls into the house. Elizabeth was unresponsive.

Gwen was devastated. This was definitely the worst birthday ever. And she had seen the faces of the police and her neighbors. Eve was right. They were not heroes. They were freaks.

****

It had been a week since the incident with the Newmans. Michelle's eye was healing, although it was still discolored. She had taken two weeks off work, while the girls took a week off from school. None of them wanted to face their peers and answer questions concerning the Newman incident.

"What do you mean *how do we feel*, Dad?" responded Eve to her father's question, as they all sat down for dinner in the formal dining room. Eve's life was unraveling. She had been imprisoned in the house for a week. The Parker sisters were not allowed to use social media (one of the few areas that her parents and grandmother agreed on), but Ana always kept them abreast of what was being said about them online. Eve had always been well-known if not well-liked, but the negative comments associated with her had been on the rise since her breakup with Tyler and had spiked again after the Newman incident. And Ana told her another company was delving into their background, so extra precautions were needed. Yet still their father would not come clean about his and David's involvement in all this.

"I mean, how do you feel about the altercation? Right in our front yard. Right in front of God and everybody."

"How should we feel? We don't feel good about it, but what else could we do?"

"Eve, what your father is trying to say is that we have to be more careful. Mr. Newman was seriously injured and it could easily have been much worse."

"So? Why should we care about Mr. Newman? He didn't care about his wife! He didn't care about Elizabeth! And he definitely didn't care about you or Gwen!"

"Eve, we have to be honest about our situation—" Barry interjected.

"Honest! Really! Well honestly, this is not our fault! Right, Dad? Honestly, we didn't ask for this! Honestly, we just want to be normal!"

Barry pounded the table. "Young lady, you need to lower your voice when talking to me!"

Eve pounded the table as well. "Lowering my voice will not fix anything! Anything! Our lives are ruined!"

Ana and Gwen sat silence while looking down at their plates.

"Eve, be patient, sweetheart. We will figure this out," Michelle interceded.

"Mom, you don't know what we've been through! You don't know how hard this is!" Eve had tears streaming down her face. Tyler was wrong; there was nothing perfect about her family.

"You're right, I don't know. I can't possibly know. But I know this…" Michelle got up and walked around the table to Eve. "I know that I love you more than anything. I know—"

"Mom, I just want to go back to the way things were. I just want to be normal again." Eve stood and clung to her mother like a life preserver.

Michelle whispered, "Eve, I promise you—me and your father are working day and night to fix this, and as a family we will overcome this. Together."

****

What a joke! Eve thought, as her cousins, father, and uncle made small talk. Everyone was talking about everything except what they needed to talk about. Eve was happy for Walter but that was not why they were here. They were here because everyone was saying she and Gwen had almost killed someone, and that they had some genetic disorder that prevented them from playing sports. Both of which were true from an academic standpoint.

"So, no press conference, nephew?" Barry teased his oldest nephew, Walter. Walter was standing next to his father, Barry's oldest brother, Benjamin. Father and son were a mirror image of each other.

Both dark-skinned, bald-headed, broad-shouldered, and impossibly muscled. The most notable difference being that Benjamin, at five feet and eleven inches, was two inches taller than his oldest son. Benjamin also sported a thick mustache in contrast to his clean-shaven son.

"Not my style, unc," Walter said, in a deep baritone. His large hands were resting on Gwen's shoulders as she stood in front of him. Eve wanted to scream. None of this was real. Her father knew it, her uncle knew it, and her cousins knew it.

"I knew you were going to Big State!" Gwen said "Your running style is perfect for their offense!"

"Remember, don't tell anyone until I announce it Monday, Gwenny. Only other people that know are my coaches."

"I'm going pro after I graduate!" Emmitt chimed in. Emmitt was Walter's younger brother. He had the same wide shoulders and big hands of his brother and father but was thin, brown-skinned, with baby dreadlocks and, at six feet five, the tallest person in the family.

"Please! You know you can't go left!" Antonio smacked Emmitt in the back of the head. Emmitt spun around and Antonio slapped him lightly across the cheek so fast it was hard to follow.

"Keep it up, punk!" Emmitt grabbed Antonio.

"Knock it off!" Benjamin's voice reverberated throughout. The boys stopped wrestling.

"He started it, Pops." Emmitt said, sullenly.

Antonio was grinning ear to ear and still in Emmitt's face. At six feet two he gave up a few inches to Emmitt, but his strong, athletic build was dripping with intensity.

"Save it for the game!" Walter stared at Antonio until Antonio let the air out of his chest and backed away from Emmitt.

Benjamin placed his massive hand on Barry's shoulder. "I better get these boys to the game, baby bruh, before they make me put my hands on 'em. So, is there anything I can do? Everything going to be OK with the girls? With you?"

"Don't worry about the girls, Benj. We just taking some extra precautions is all," Barry replied, taking off his glasses and cleaning them on his shirt.

Antonio approached Eve. "I'm sorry, cuz. I... I was really looking forward to you doing that spin move in games. We going to get home late after the game, but I still want you to call me, OK?"

Eve nodded because she didn't trust herself to talk. Antonio grabbed her for a few seconds and then gently released her.

I'm not going to cry! I'm not going to cry! Eve thought, biting her lip.

"Boys, let's hit it. Tip-off is in an hour and I told coach I'd have you there early." Benjamin grabbed Barry in a tight embrace. "Anything you need, baby bruh, you call. OK?"

"Thanks, Benj. I will." Benjamin, Walter, Emmitt, and Antonio climbed into the SUV and pulled away.

"Let's finish the game," Eve said, after their father had gone inside. She needed to do something; standing still was driving her crazy.

"Cool." Gwen retrieved the ball and tossed it to her.

Eve cradled the ball and eyed Gwen. When Gwen reached for the ball, Eve spun around her for an easy layup.

147

The next play, Gwen got physical.

"Foul!" Eve slapped Gwen's hand away.

"Stop crying and play ball, Princess! Unlike you, me and Ana get cold." Gwen did have a point. Both she and Ana were in sweatshirts and jogging pants. Eve was wearing a T-shirt and shorts. It didn't matter how cold it was, the weather never bothered Eve.

"Stop fouling me and I will!"

"If you…" Gwen started to say, but Eve spun around her again. Gwen chased her down, swatting away her layup from behind. Eve was knocked to the ground in the process.

"You did that on purpose!" Eve shouted, jumping up.

Gwen ignored her as she grabbed the ball.

Eve ran and pushed Gwen from behind, as hard as she could. The effect was jarring. Eve's teeth rattled as she stopped dead in her tracks.

"Stop tickling me!" Gwen laughed.

Eve kicked Gwen in the back of her knee. Gwen dropped the ball and her hands flew up as she fell to the ground.

"You're dead, Princess!" Gwen shouted, jumping up.

"Come on!" Eve shouted back at her as they circled each other. Eve started bouncing on her toes. Gwen stopped circling and set her feet. Eve and Gwen had sparred over a thousand times the last few months. With no basketball, Tae Kwon Do, or any other school activity to occupy their time, it was pretty much all they did. The upside to all that sparring and working out was knowing each other's weak points. The downside to all that sparring and working out was knowing each other's weak points.

"Hey!" they shouted in unison, as Ana sprayed them with the garden hose.

"We don't have time for this!" Ana scolded them. "We're going live in two weeks! Two weeks!"

Eve and Gwen stared at Ana. Eve didn't know why, but she started laughing. Once she started she couldn't stop. She was joined by Gwen.

"Geez, Super Dork. I wasn't going to hurt her," Gwen struggled to say.

"This isn't funny! Two weeks! We only have two weeks to get ready!" Ana repeated.

Eve held out her dripping arms and walked toward Ana. "C'mere, Ana; you need a hug."

"Eww! No! Get away!" Ana shouted, running away.

"Wow! I never seen Super Dork move so fast!"

A soaked Eve put an arm around Gwen. "Come on, sis, let's work on your crossover."

Chapter 11

Gwen watched Rebecca stare at her with her mouth opening and closing like she was trying to figure out how it worked. Finally, Rebecca said, "What's up with the new security guard?"

"He's, uh, different," Toni noted, looking over her shoulder at him.

"Like this place needs more security," Gwen offered between bites, as she glanced at the security guard. He had started working at the school the same time as the new janitor. He was there because of her. Gwen knew he was biding his time—making a note of her schedule and her friends.

"Uh, Gwen, I bet he's here just to keep an eye on you. Everybody knows you and Melissa are planning to do something before the school year is out." Toni laughed.

Gwen shook her head. "Can I just offer that the administration's decision to reallocate much-needed funds on unnecessary security really speaks volumes to the value system of the leadership in this school, and I pray for the children."

"You're back!" Rebecca said, drawing a sharp look from Toni that was not missed by Gwen.

"What do you mean?"

"Well, you know… It's just that you haven't been yourself, lately. And you've been missing a lot of school and… And, you know, since you and Eve beat down Elizabeth's dad…" Rebecca mumbled.

"Everyone's worried about you, Gwen," Toni cut in. "Is everything OK with you, Eve, and Ana?"

"What? We're fine! Parents just overprotective, is all."

Rebecca seemed oblivious to the sharp stares from Toni and Dana as she soldiered on. "You going to the dance this Saturday, then? You think Elizabeth might show up? Has anyone heard from her?"

Gwen got up with her tray. "Can't make the dance. Going to my Grams' for the weekend. You know, family stuff."

Toni got up as well. "Yeah, me and Dana were talking about not going, either."

"But Tyler is DJ'ing!" offered Rebecca, as she followed Gwen, Toni, and Dana.

"Yeah, I heard." Gwen took one last bite of her apple and tossed it toward the trash can.

"Gwendolyn Parker, you missed," the security guard said, pointing to the apple core on the floor.

"Oh, I'm sorry." Gwen picked up the apple core and put it in the trash can.

The security guard grabbed her wrist, and whispered, "I thought you'd be bigger." Surprised, Gwen snatched it away, and the security guard voluntarily let go. With no resistance, Gwen stumbled and fell.

Everyone in the cafeteria noticed. Laughter ensued from the table that Javier was sitting at. Jeff made sure everyone noticed, by clapping and pointing at Gwen.

"Gwen!" laughed Toni, as Gwen got up slowly while looking at the smirking security guard.

"I'm fine. I'm OK. Just slipped." Gwen studied the security guard more closely. He was of medium height and build with a slightly protruding stomach. His uniform was clean, his shoes polished. He could be in his early twenties. His pale skin was pockmarked and his black, thinning hair was slicked back. But there was more to him than met the eyes. He was strong; too strong.

As Gwen left the cafeteria, the conversations faded into the background. That had been intentional. That was a message that said, "We can get you at any time." Picking up her pace, Gwen got a spark in her eye and a determined look. She caught herself clenching her fist and forced her hand open while the tension migrated to shoulders. *Game on!* she thought.

****

Eve examined Gwen as they stood at her locker after school. She was biting her lip to prevent her temper, which was always close to the surface, from bubbling over. "The security guard assaulted you?"

"No! It wasn't an assault! It was a message! I think we need to postpone this weekend and deal with the security guard and janitor first. What if they know?"

"No! No way! We are going forward with this! Ana, what did you find out about them?" No more excuses for Eve, it was time to act.

"They are not employees of the school, but contractors. The company that pays them is a shell company based in the Caymans."

"That's it?" Gwen asked.

"This is not easy! They are obviously accustomed to covering their tracks. I'm working on it but it's going to take more time. And

152

Gwen might have a point. Maybe we should do more discovery on these two before we proceed."

"Ana, you were the one who told us our condition was grave! You were the one who told us you could fix it! You were the one who told us to trust you! And now you tell us we should wait! Wait for what? To die? To get kidnapped! To get experimented on? I'm not waiting! I'm tired of being scared. I'm tired of always looking over my shoulder. I'm going to do this with or without you two." Eve held her chin up. She wanted this over and didn't care what she had to do to end it.

Gwen and Ana looked at each other. Ana said, "OK. But I have a lot to do before Saturday."

Gwen shook her head. "OK, Eve, calm down, jeez. We'll do it, but I want it noted for the record that I have a sixth sense about these things and this doesn't feel right!"

***

"Are you sure they're asleep?" Gwen whispered to Ana, as they quietly left the house with their bikes.

"Yes."

"Do you think they suspected anything? Mom mentioned the wine tasted different," Gwen said, riding next to Ana.

"Maybe, but my options were limited. Plus, I didn't realize mother had such a refined taste for wine."

"Grams owns a vineyard. Every year they visit wineries in France. Isn't that something you should have factored in?" Eve added, as they entered the park and headed for the camouflaged tarp.

Ana didn't respond.

It was dark, with a patches of fog. Once they were in the park, the full moon provided enough light to change clothes.

"Hurry. Ahmed should be waiting for us." Ana said, as they left their bikes under the tarp.

"Ana, these outfits are much better. I'm definitely keeping this," Eve said, while admiring her skintight designer jeans. Due to her small waist and the size of her butt, Eve could not find high-end designer jeans to fit her. And even if she could, her mother (who was more conscious of perceptions then she let on) would not buy them for her. Eve's aunt was the person responsible for supplying her with all her high-end clothes. Twisting and turning to look at herself in her jeans, Eve also appreciated the knee-high soft leather riding boots, silk off-white blouse, and black leather half-jacket. Her oversized soft leather tote bag was the perfect accessory and matched her boots.

"They OK. Not really my style, though," Gwen noted, as she pulled on her black jean jacket, which matched her jeans. Still walking, Gwen checked the contents of her backpack and pulled out the same wig she'd worn at the hospital.

They made the ten minute walk to school in silence. Two minutes later, Ahmed arrived, grinning. "Yes, yes Ms. Pink, Ms. Green, Ms. Black, so good to see you again. I'm on time, right? So we go to mall, yes?"

"Yes, Ahmed," Ana said.

Ahmed let them off in front of the mall. "OK, two hours. Yes, yes? I be back in two hours. Yes? Have fun!" a cheery Ahmed said, as he took the money from Ana.

When Ahmed drove off, Gwen put on a cowboy hat that she pulled from her backpack.

"Hold out your hands, Gwen," Ana instructed. Gwen complied and Ana squeezed a clear gel into her hands. "Rub it in thoroughly."

Gwen fastidiously rubbed the gel on her hands and face.

"It feels like glue," she noted. When she'd finished, Ana expertly applied a fake mustache and beard. "Now give it a few seconds."

Gwen shifted her weight from one foot to the other while Ana and Eve stared at her.

"That is amazing!" Eve said, after a few seconds.

Ana looked at Gwen's now-weathered face and hands. With her mustache and beard she could pass for a forty-year-old man.

"I feel ridiculous, and this stuff itches!" Gwen complained.

"I think you look fine, sweetheart!" Eve mocked, while putting on a blonde wig and large designer glasses.

"You look good, Gwen," Ana said, while sagging her baggy jeans and putting on an oversized football jersey. After putting on a do-rag, Ana tipped her baseball cap to the side and pulled it down over her eyes before putting her backpack on again.

"Well, I guess we better get going." Eve sighed as they emerged from the parked cars. She watched the bustling activity surrounding them: parents were corralling unruly children; teenage sweethearts were holding hands; prides of adolescent boys were walking, texting, and laughing; and teenage girls were giggling and talking over each other. Eve had never felt so out of place and alone.

"Come on, junior," Gwen said to Ana, as she followed Eve.

155

The "family" of husband, wife, and son walked six blocks. They were invisible to the hurried, upscale crowd; people walked around them with their Macy's shopping bags or looked through them to window shop. The frenetic activity amid the buildings of the commercial section gradually decreased. Eventually they were alone in front of a large, ostentatious pharmaceutical building. The building was as intimidating as it was grand. It was surrounded by a twelve foot spiked iron gate, with a small guard shack outside the fence, facing the sprawling parking lot.

Ana looked the building up and down and adjusted her single strap backpack.

"We can change over there." Eve pointed to a set of trees outside the gate

"Cool," Gwen added, pulling off her fake mustache, beard, and weathered skin in one piece.

Using the largest tree as cover, they changed clothes. Under their full clothes, they were already wearing black, full-bodied leotards of Ana's design. They put on black military pants, Kevlar vests, knee pads, elbow pads, and black baseball caps. Ana and Eve put on combat boots; Gwen already had her boots on.

"Now, this is what I'm talking about! This is some superhero stuff right here!" Gwen said, while looking herself over. She secured the rope that was draped diagonally across her body, then she adjusted her knee and elbow pads. "Where you get all this stuff from?"

"The boots, vests, and pads are standard SWAT issue. The leotard is all mine. It's a derivative of Kevlar that I've been playing with.

It's light, flexible, fire resistant, and bulletproof, all while allowing the body to breathe. The patent is pending."

"Cool!"

"Anyway...let me run a couple of checks before we get started." Ana pulled out a paper-thin electronic pad.

"Ms. Green, that is the coolest thing I've ever seen! What is it, a computer? A tablet?"

"Well, it should be the world's most powerful handheld computer. I designed the specs myself. I keep it synced with our earpieces and phones.

"OK, from this point on, only use our code names. Ms. Pink, once I say 'Go' you have seven seconds to get over the fence and to the wall. Remember to hug the wall as tightly as possible. It's the only blind spot inside the fence. And go easy on the guard. I thought you were unnecessarily rough in the hospital."

"Whatever. We got out, didn't we? And please just toss me over the fence not the building, Ms. Black! You kept throwing me too high in practice."

Gwen nodded.

Eve hugged and fist-bumped her sisters. She walked off twenty feet away from the fence. Gwen crawled on her stomach to the bushes next to the fence.

"I can only run interference for seven seconds, so be quick. Now wait for my signal." Ana looked at the computer and held her left arm up.

"Wait!" Eve shouted.

"Is everything cool? We don't have to go through with this. We can figure something else out." Gwen said.

"No! We are doing this! Just nervous, is all. I'm ready now." Eve got in a sprinter stance, looking straight ahead. She was determined and focused. *It's about to get real!* She thought.

Ana raised her hand. Eve could feel her heart beating against her chest. Her mouth went dry.

"Go!" Ana shouted, bringing her arm down. Simultaneously, Eve and Gwen started running. Gwen reached her spot against the fence first. She turned to face Eve with her hands cupped together below her waist. Eve ran full speed at Gwen. Two steps away from her sister, Eve leaped. She placed a foot in Gwen's cupped hands. Gwen tossed Eve up while Eve jumped. She was airborne.

She was near the top of the fence when she panicked. The angle was wrong; she was going to be impaled on the spikes. A flash of heat and everything stopped moving. Eve contorted her body. Slowly, everything started moving again. Eve barely avoided the spikes as she passed over the fence. As her descent sped up she twisted, turned, and flipped. She landed feet first, collapsed into a forward roll, and sprinted toward the wall.

"Oh! My! God! That was the most incredible thing I have ever seen! It's like you were an Olympic gymnast!" Gwen exclaimed through the earpiece.

"Those were some absolutely stunning moves. How do you feel now?" Ana added.

"Good. I'll meet you guys by the guard shack." Eve controlled her breathing. *So far so good,* she thought. With any luck they would get the materials, Ana would make the antidote, and they could mark "stop impending death" off their to-do list. Then they would deal with the security guard and janitor and whomever they worked for.

****

"I'm ready!" Gwen heard Eve say through her earpiece.

Wonderful! Gwen thought. She hated that she'd let Eve convince them to go forward when she knew better. She, however, was not going to let Eve take any unnecessary risks; it was time she saved her big sister from herself.

Ana distracted Gwen by typing. That the girl could type so fast on a tablet was amazing. A second later a song started blaring out of the tablet that carried over the parking lot and toward the guard shack.

We're no strangers to love,

You know the rules and so do I...

A few seconds later the guard came out. He looked around as Ana and Gwen watched from behind a car. Gwen saw Eve sneak up behind him and kick him in the back of his knee; he fell immediately. Before he had a chance to scream out, Eve deftly applied a rear naked choke. With his carotid artery prevented from supplying blood to his brain the guard passed out.

Never gonna give you up,

Never gonna let you down...

"OK, now please turn that off!" Gwen shouted, as Eve opened up the fence from inside the guard shack.

We've known each other for so long,

Your heart's been aching but you're too shy to say it...

Ana turned off the music. "You really don't like it? It's Rick Astley's 'Never Gonna Give You Up.' It's a classic."

Gwen grabbed the guard as he was coming to. She quickly taped his hands together behind his back and then his feet. She applied a blindfold, taped his mouth shut, and put soundproof headphones on him. The headphones played "Never Gonna Give You Up" over and over, courtesy of Ana.

After plugging her computer in, Ana checked all the security cameras on the console in the guard shack. The floor plans of all thirty-six floors flashed by in less than a minute. She stared intently at the images.

The images flashed by too fast for Gwen to focus. "Uh, Ms. Green, what are you doing"

"I'm memorizing the floor plans. I couldn't find any up-to-date specs online."

"Good to know."

"OK, got it." Ana started typing onto her pad. Ten seconds later, everything went black. Street lights, traffic lights, building lights. Everything. Seconds later, a few floors lit up in the building.

"What did you do? What just happened?" Eve demanded.

"I crashed the energy grid for this quadrant," Ana said calmly. Stepping outside the guard shack, she slowly looked the building up and down twice through a small scope.

Gwen looked at Eve. Eve shrugged her shoulders and adjusted her rope. "OK, I'll bite… and why did you crash the energy grid for this quadrant?"

"The building is now being powered by backup generators. But the generators have a limited capacity, so only the floors that are most critical to the business should be on," Ana explained, as a 3D rendering of the building materialized above her tablet. The rendering contained small human images inside. "The outage will only last seven minutes, but when the power comes back on the cameras will be in an endless loop, so we don't have to worry about being seen. Now, the lobby security will be checking every floor, so we need to check our five floors as quickly as possible. I already unlocked the doors to the loading dock, so let's go! Wait…"

Gwen saw that Ana had a concerned look on her face. "What's wrong?"

"They have a larger janitorial staff than I figured. I count nine individuals in the building, but—"

"But what?" Gwen pressed.

"Heat signature. There is something different, unique, about one of the heat signatures. We might want to rethink this."

"See, I told you! It's a trap!"

"You don't know that! We have to try. We have to at least try. I can't go on like this!"

"Fine, Eve! Fine! But I'm only going in if we're not doing the stupid monster movie thing and splitting up. We check the floors together."

161

"No. That'll take too long," Eve stated.

"Can't you see something is wrong here? I have a sixth sense about these things and this doesn't feel right! So we go in together and stay together or we don't go in!"

"OK, fine, whatever."

"Cool. And another thing—" Gwen started, before Eve interrupted her.

"Wait! Shouldn't we say a prayer first or something?"

"You can't be serious!"

"Why wouldn't I be serious?"

"We're about to break into a building! And you just choked out a security guard. Doesn't it say in the Bible, 'Thou shalt not choke out minimum wage workers'?"

"Don't get an attitude! I'm just saying—a prayer might be nice!"

"You can't pray before you break into a building! Plus, that guy probably has a wife and kids! Now he's going to lose his job because he was choked out by a bookworm! I pray that you don't run into another security guard or janitor!"

"You're not funny! Let's just go!"

"Wait, here, take these. You can hook them on your belt." Ana gave Eve and Gwen some canisters.

Eve inspected one of the canisters. "What are they?"

"Tear gas."

Gwen clipped her canisters on her belt. "Anyway, remember if something happens we go out the windows and not the exits. That's what the ropes are for. Got it?"

"Can we do this already?" Eve stormed off.

Gwen stood over Ana as Ana slid a card through an electronic door reader.

"What is that card again?" The girls were in a dimly lit hallway. Abstract artwork adorned the walls and the floors were polished marble. Ana was attempting to open two large double doors.

"It's a skeleton key. It has integrated circuits and a microprocessor that communicates wirelessly with my computer. The first swipe detects the type of cryptography or encryption algorithm, and voila! The second swipe unlocks the door. It works on hotel rooms too!"

"Are you two finished? Can we go in now?" Eve asked, as the door opened. The three sisters entered cautiously. The room had a large a lab at the center, surrounded by cubicles. The lab was encased in glass with a biohazard sign on the door. Two large oak desks were directly in front of the lab door.

"This must be it!" Eve exclaimed

"Wait, I thought I heard something?" Gwen whispered.

"You kept saying that on the sixth floor. I'm not falling for it," Eve replied.

"I keep telling you, this doesn't feel right. And where are all those janitors?"

"Hmm. That's actually a good point…" Ana noted.

Click, click.

The girls froze. Holding her breath, Gwen noted the east and west ends were a wall of windows. The west side was too far away. Plus they would have to pass an emergency exit. Gwen grabbed her rope and started walking toward the east windows.

"Come on! We have to go!" she whispered to Ana and Eve, who were still frozen. She came back for them. "Ana, lock the doors, and let's go!"

She started pushing them toward the windows. She stopped when she heard footsteps outside the door they'd just come in. She heard more footsteps coming up the stairwell of the emergency exit. Whoever they were, they'd given up the pretense of being quiet.

"Ana! Lock the doors! Lock the doors!" Gwen was shaking Ana.

"OK, OK," Ana replied, pulling away. Hands trembling, she started typing on her computer. A second later, Gwen heard the locks slide in place on the large double doors and a click on the emergency door. "OK, every door in the building is locked—"

Ana's voice was cut off by someone trying to open the large door. Someone else attempted to open the emergency exit. Gwen pushed Eve and Ana toward the window.

Boom! Boom! Something slammed against the double doors.

"Get to the window!" Gwen yelled at her sisters. Eve turned into a blur. She solidified at the window and started tying off her rope around a column.

Gwen pushed over one of the large desks, moving it against the double doors. The desk was old and solidly built. *It must weigh over two hundred pounds*, Gwen thought, *and should buy us a few extra minutes.*

The emergency door was flung open. Gwen hurled the other desk at it. Spinning through the air, the desk hit a man in the chest as he stepped through the doorway. He bounced off the wall and hit the floor face first. He groaned but didn't get up. The desk was now wedged tightly in the doorway. Another man must have jumped down the stairwell to avoid it. Gwen heard him scream when he landed. *Probably a broken a leg*, she thought. A third man cried out softly for help. He was pinned between the door and the wall. The desk was securely wedged in the doorway, creating a trap. He couldn't move, and from the sound of his cries he could barely breathe.

Boom! Boom! The other desk was moving with each boom. A few more hits and they would be inside the room.

Running, Gwen took out two tear gas grenades. She pulled the pins with her mouth and threw them over her shoulder. Ana and Eve were trying to break the window with a chair, but had only managed a spiderweb crack.

Boom! Boom! Gwen heard the door open behind her.

"Grab your ropes! Grab your ropes!" she yelled.

Running full speed, Gwen scooped up Ana, tossing her over her shoulder. With her free hand, she snatched Eve by the back of her collar. Still running, she put her head down and launched herself at the window.

Gwen crashed through the window. Letting go of her sisters she fell seven stories. She managed to say every prayer she had ever learned. She even made up a few before hitting the ground and landing on her back.

Cool! The full moon is beautiful tonight, she thought, looking up. Her sisters were staring down at her. Their mouths and faces looked like they were shouting. Gwen smiled at them. She had never seen Ana so animated. *I could really go for a big plate of ribs right now,* Gwen thought.

Eve started shaking Gwen, shouting "Gwen! Gwen!"

Gradually, Gwen started coming to her senses. When she finally realized their situation, she staggered to her feet, shouting, "I'm fine! I'm fine! Run! Don't stop, go! Go!"

Her sisters obliged.

Ana was talking very fast into her phone as she ran.

"Ahmed will meet us two blocks up in three minutes!"

Ana and Eve both stopped to climb the fence.

"We don't have time for that! Ana set off the emergency alarm, fire alarm, bad breath alarm, whatever else kind of alarm you can in that building!" Gwen yelled. The cobwebs were gone. Picking up speed, she rammed her shoulder into the gate. A portion of the fence fell to a forty-five degree angle. The girls scampered onto it and jumped down.

Ana typed while running, and alarms started going off inside the building.

"Give me your tear gas!" Gwen shouted.

"Gwen, I'm the fastest!" Eve shouted back.

Ana pointed toward the window they'd just escaped from. "Look!"

Gwen turned and saw a figure looking out the broken window partially blurred by the tear gas smoke that was streaming out. The figure jumped.

"Go! I'm right behind you." Gwen took the grenades and pushed her sisters. She ran back toward the fence throwing grenades at the building. After three grenades, the smoke mixed with the fog reduced visibility to three feet.

"Gwen! Gwen! Where are you? We're here with Ahmed!" Eve said in her earpiece.

"I'm coming. I'm coming!" Gwen was coughing and wheezing. Confused, she attempted to backtrack her steps. She heard a car horn to her right. She also heard something move behind her. She threw her last grenade in the direction of the movement and took off toward the horn. She traveled twenty feet before she could see her hands in front of her face. Coughing and wheezing, she started running hard.

"Gwen! Gwen! Where are you? I'm coming!" Eve screamed in her earpiece.

"No! I'm almost there!"

Ten more feet and she saw the cab. Her sisters were beside it. She heard police sirens and the horn of a fire truck, but couldn't figure out which direction they were coming from. She broke into a full sprint. Diving into the backseat, she shouted, "Step on it!"

"Yes. Yes, Ms. Black."

Chapter 12

"Any more bright ideas, genius?" The moon was still bright and the night was still damp and foggy. The girls were riding their bikes through the park on their way home.

"Give it a rest, Gwen." Eve said, before adding, "Do you think we should have changed?" The girls hadn't talked much since they'd escaped from the pharmaceutical building thirty minutes earlier. The silence and stillness of the park was unnerving.

"Naw. I'm too tired. Besides, Band Geek said Mom and Dad should still be out cold."

"Good point. All I want to do is get home and crawl into bed. How are your eyes?"

"OK. Throat's still a little scratchy, though. Hey, who is that at the basketball court? The park is closed."

The girls stopped as two men on the basketball court approached them. Glancing around, Eve saw three more men positioning themselves directly behind her. She didn't panic; she nodded to her sisters, they nodded back, and dismounted. There would be no more running tonight.

Eve recognized the janitor by his height and gait. A second later she realized he was with the new security guard. The janitor stood off to one side of Gwen, while the security guard positioned himself near Ana. Eve didn't like this; she was going to need to take out the three men behind her as quickly as possible to help Ana. Gwen should be OK.

"Ah! The Parker sisters! We didn't think you'd make it out the building. But here you are." The school security guard spoke in a cheery tone. He was still in his uniform, as was the janitor.

Eve didn't respond. She looked at the three men behind her again. They were dressed in what appeared to be brand-new camouflaged clothes and boots. She didn't recognize them but their body language and clothes told her everything she needed to know. *Rookies,* she thought. They were standing too close together. No spacing. And they were fidgeting. They reminded Eve of the first time she and Gwen had gone out for basketball. They stayed at each other's side the entire practice. These three had that same look.

"Yes. Like I said, it is in indoub, doub… It is in, indoob bee lee…" the security guard stuttered, before Gwen interrupted him.

"Are you trying to say indubitably? I don't think that word means what you think it means."

"Young lady, do you not realize how malicious your situation is"

"Dude, you're killing me! Do you mean precarious? Is there another evil henchman we can talk to? It sounds like this could take a while and it's past our bedtime."

"Shut up! Just shut your mouth!"

"Hey! I understood that!"

"Gwen." Eve nodded at the three men behind her. They were now holding guns. Eve couldn't believe how calm they were all behaving given their current predicament. *That's just how the Parker sisters roll!* She laughed to herself but this was no laughing matter, and she started thinking about what had to happen for them to get home safely.

"No guns! No guns!" The security guard shouted. "If the merchandise is in any way injured, I will have your hides!"

Ana yawned. "Excuse me, Mr. Willis? Would you be so kind as to tell us what your intentions are? My sister is right; it is rather late for us, so anything you can do to hurry this along would be appreciated."

"Ana! Yes, Ana! I understand you are the genius, correct? Well, indoob, indoubely. In doob bee. We just need a blood sample. It should only take a minute and you can be on your way. I'm sure you understand?"

"I'm sorry, Mr. Willis, or whatever your real name is. You won't be getting a blood sample today," Eve replied.

"Well, indoob, in doob bee belie—" Mr. Willis started, before Gwen interrupted him again.

"Jeez, we surrender! Just stop trying to say that word!"

"Gwen. Please let him finish." Eve wanted this over tonight.

"Well. Let me start again. My employer would like to have a blood sample. He also requests your permission to undergo a few follow-up tests and uh, un-invensive processes. At your earliest convenience, of course."

"Do you mean noninvasive procedures? My God, man; get it together!"

Looking over her shoulder briefly, Eve made a note of how close the three men were to her and how close they were to each other. She started visualizing her attack while addressing Mr. Willis. "So your employer wants our cooperation to run tests and take blood. And your employer is asking instead of kidnapping us because of our grandmother

170

and the resources at her disposal. Otherwise we would already be on a milk carton. Risking exposure if something happened to the granddaughters of Josephine is not something your employer is willing to do."

"How very receptive of you. Yes, we were told to be patient with you and give you a bit of leeway because of the statue of your family. But make no mistake—we do not get paid unless we deliver. And we always deliver."

"It's perceptive and status! Somebody make him stop! I can't take this anymore!"

"Young lady, that will be enough of that! I am tired of your in, incorrible attitude!"

Eve felt movement behind her. A flash of heat and everything stopped. Spinning around, she saw her three assailants were frozen. She liver-kicked the first man and then did a front snap kick to his knee. She heard the bone snap. Taking his gun from its holster she tossed it aside. Spinning away, she came up between the open arms of the second man.

Faster! Faster! Eve thought.

She struck the second man's nose with her palm in an upward motion, and felt the cartilage give way. Everything was slowly starting to move again. Swinging her arms forward, she popped his ears with her open palms and grabbed his gun. Throwing his gun aside, she kicked him under his chin, lifting him off the ground. Everything was almost back to regular speed.

No! Not yet! Not! Yet! Eve shouted to herself.

She turned just as the third man threw a punch. She slipped it. Grabbing his fist, she pulled it toward her while striking the back of his elbow with her open palm. His arm snapped. Still moving, she did a spinning heel kick while grabbing his gun. The kick connected in the back of his head, and the force sent him falling. Eve spun again, hitting him in the same spot in the back of his head with the butt of his gun to accelerate his fall. Eve dropped the gun.

"Ug! Heh! Heh!" The first man dropped to the fetal position. Discombobulated from the liver kick, he tried to reach for his busted leg but gave up.

The second man landed with a loud thud on his back. His nose spraying blood, he turned on his side and passed out.

The last man fell to the ground like a tree and did not move.

Out of breath, Eve checked for her sisters. It had taken her less than two seconds to dispatch her three adversaries but a lot could happen in that time.

"Are you not entertained?" Gwen shouted. She had the janitor in a headlock. She was delivering punch after punch. The sound reverberated through the park.

Ana was sitting on the back of Mr. Willis, who was face down in the grass. She had his arm twisted behind his back. His shoulder looked dislocated.

"Put him down! And make sure he stays!" Eve shouted to Gwen, while catching her breath.

Gwen snatched the janitor up by his ponytail and punched him in the stomach. He doubled over. She uppercut him so hard it sounded like a car crash. The punch lifted the janitor four feet in the air and deposited him five feet away. He hit the ground, tried to stand up, and stumbled back down. Gwen pretended to brush dirt off her shoulder.

Eve surveyed the damage. Her three men were still down: one was coughing and spitting up blood as his nose bled profusely; one was still out cold with a grotesquely twisted arm; and one struggled to stand on a broken leg. He looked at Eve and reached for his gun a few feet away.

"Gwen." Eve pointed at the man.

"Way ahead of ya, sis." Gwen rushed past Eve. She grabbed the hand that had been reaching for the gun. Two distinct snaps were heard, like logs popping on a fire. "Oops! Sorry about that. Adrenaline, you know."

"Ah! Ahhh! My fingers!"

Eve winced. She'd never heard a man scream so loud.

"Uh, Gwen?" Eve was afraid his screaming was loud enough to reach a couple of the nearby houses.

Gwen nodded as she forcefully duct taped his mouth.

Pushing him back down, Gwen picked up his gun. Grunting, she bent the gun, rendering it useless. She repeated this with the other two weapons.

Eve looked at the fallen bodies. "We're good." She then walked over to Mr. Willis while Ana got off him. Whimpering, he didn't look up. Kneeling down, Eve grabbed him roughly by the hair with one hand. She grabbed his throat with the other and slowly squeezed. She was tired.

So tired. She wanted this to be over. Eve barely noticed when his eyes rolled to the back of his head.

"Eve, stop it, you're killing him. Stop it!" She heard Ana say.

"Let him go, Eve." Gwen added, putting a hand on her shoulder.

Eve released his throat. He gasped for air. She wiped her tears with the back of her hand. Still holding his hair, she made him look at her. "If you come near me or my family again, I will kill you. Then I will find your boss and kill him."

The girls got on their bikes and rode home. They didn't look back.

***

Gwen was drilling Ana Monday morning before school.

"Ana, we know he came at you! But how did you dislocate his shoulder and get him down?"

"I told you. I didn't dislocate his shoulder. He did. I'll show you tonight when we spar. I got the move off the Internet."

"Ana, Gwen's right. You're not making any sense. This guy was supposed to be strong. Real strong. And you disposed of him with something you learned online? Explain it again."

"OK. The janitor went after Gwen."

"You already said that. Get back to Mr. Indubitably," Gwen said impatiently.

"He attacked from a traditional boxing stance. So I ruled out kicks. And getting me out of commission quickly would free him up to assist with you or Eve. That left an overhand right as the most probable strike from that distance—"

"So you guessed?" Gwen interrupted her.

"No, I didn't guess! I calculated all the probable options and deduced the most likely. I'm not as fast as Eve or as strong as you. My only chance was to anticipate. So I slipped his punch, stepped on his foot, and pulled his arm behind him as he fell. The trick was holding his arm at the right angle when he hit the ground."

"I'm sorry. I fell asleep. Were you still talking? So, long story short... you guessed."

"Never mind."

Eve looked at both her sisters. "What are we going to do now?"

Gwen and Ana went silent and looked down.

"Ana?" Eve persisted.

"I have an idea. But we are going to need an adult. I think. I'm still working on it."

"When was the last time you guys had a nosebleed?"

"About two weeks," Ana answered.

"Same. And you?" Gwen replied

"This morning. And a headache." Eve lowered her voice

Gwen looked up with red eyes. "Eve?"

"You guys know how lucky we are, right?"

Ana and Gwen gave her blank stares.

"How many countries have we been to? How many times have we ridden in Gram's private jet just to go to Disneyland?"

"Yeah. I get it. You're talking about Tyler," Gwen mumbled.

"No. Well yeah, I guess I am. But not just Tyler. Lucia too. And Harold."

Ana looked up at Eve. "Who's Harold?"

"The old janitor. His name is Harold. Whoever Lurch and the security guard works for got him fired so they could take his place. He lives alone. No wife, no kids, and now no job. But you know, it's not really about the money. Elizabeth has money."

"What exactly are you saying?"

"I don't know, Ana. But I'm tired of being mad. I'm tired of feeling sorry for myself. I don't know how long we have, but does anyone? And what would change if we did? We've been blessed with everything and what have we done, so far? We fight each other, buy clothes, play pranks, and embezzle money."

"I never embezzled!"

"Ana, that's not the point. I get what you're saying, Eve. But we're just kids…"

"When has that ever stopped you, Gwen? And didn't you say we were blessed with extraordinary gifts? But the question is, what are we going to do with them? Maybe there is a higher purpose for us. Maybe this happened for a reason."

"What we think, we become." Ana spoke quietly.

"What?" Gwen said.

"Buddha," Ana answered.

"Well, look at you going all Buddha on everyone. But what does Buddha say about embezzling?"

"I didn't embezzle! I made that money!"

"Will you two chill? So what are we going to do now?"

"I don't know, Eve. What if I was wrong? I mean its obvious Dad's friend Dave put something in his Cheerios or something. Whether Dad agreed or not I don't know. And please believe that whatever happened was not preordained. We are dying, Eve. From the looks of it you sooner than me and Ana. What higher purpose does that serve?"

"It had to be an operation. It wasn't anything Dad would have ingested," Ana suggested.

"Seriously, Ana? Can you stay on topic?" Gwen raised her voice. "The fact is, we're just kids! We shouldn't be dealing with this by ourselves! We have to come clean. About the lab beneath the basement, about the hospital, about Lurch and the security guard. About all of it!"

"No. And let me be clear; I am not saying anything, you are not saying anything, and Ana is not saying anything. I don't know what we're dealing with but I don't want to put Mom and Dad at risk. The doctor dying still scares me." Eve was resolute.

Gwen slammed her hand down and shook the bar. "So what are we going to do then!"

"Hey! I just thought of something that might work!" Ana chimed in.

"Really?" Eve brightened.

"Yeah! But it might be risky."

"Come on, Gwen." Eve pleaded, while hugging Gwen and gently bringing their foreheads into contact. "You know you're dying to uppercut somebody again." She laughed.

"OK, OK. Count me in." Gwen tried not to smile while pushing Eve away. "Damn, girl, I got to get you some more Altoids!"

177

"Whatever!" Eve laughed. "Ana, while you put your plan in place we still need to find out who Mr. Willis and Lurch work for!"

"We will. I'm just waiting for them to make their move. I'm fairly confident after what just happened they will single one of us out fairly quick now."

"Team Parker, back in action!" Eve laughed, as their mother came down to give them a ride to school.

Chapter 13

"Anastasia! Anastasia Parker!"

Ana raised her head up and rubbed her eyes.

"Yes?"

The other students in class giggled quietly.

"You were snoring, Anastasia Parker!" Mr. Little chided.

The class laughed louder.

"OK, everyone else, pencils down and eyes forward," Mr. Little instructed, as he surveyed the class. "Now class, I know everyone absolutely hates math. But in today's fast changing world, students who do not have strong math skills will be at a distinct disadvantage. Especially when competing for the high-end jobs that separate the haves from the have-nots..." Mr. Little trailed off.

"Ana! Can you please join us? Thank you. Now wouldn't you agree, Ms. Parker?"

"Is it your contention that if we don't develop strong math skills at this juncture in our scholastic career it will forever doom us to being a have-not? You believe that without strong math skills, we would not have the requisite tools to compete in an increasingly competitive market that puts a premium on said math skills?"

Mr. Little clasped his hands together. "Yes, Ms. Parker... exactly!"

"Then I disagree..." Ana laid her head back down.

"Ms. Parker, could you please sit up? Thank you. Now, would you care to enlighten us on what you feel is the biggest indicator for a student's future success?"

"Zip code."

"I'm sorry, Ms. Parker... Could you please repeat that?"

Ana stifled a yawn. "The biggest factor to a student's future success is their zip code or what neighborhood they live in or, more accurately, their current class and status."

"Ms. Parker, could you please give me the pleasure of your undivided attention? Thank you. Now, I'm sorry, Ms. Parker, but if I am to understand you correctly you are in essence saying that hard work and effort be damned? That as long as mommy and daddy have money I'll be OK?"

"I didn't say that. You did. You asked me what was the biggest indicator of a student's future success and I said a student's current class and status. Of course, hard work and effort are also determinate factors. But class and status are easily the more accurate indicators of a student's future success if by success you mean class and status."

"Ms. Parker I have to say I'm flabbergasted and more than a bit disappointed by your answer. But I guess as someone with class and status it was easy to arrive at your thesis."

"It was."

"Ms. Parker, Ms. Parker... Again I am just flabbergasted and shocked by what I am hearing. And I would so hate to prove you wrong, but statistics and studies have shown that students who don't do well in math are at a serious disadvantage when entering the job market. I'll be happy to share these studies with you, if you like?"

"No, thanks. I'm not interested in studies or statistics based on faulty logic postulated on imperfect data collection. But I can tell you this… students that get a C in this math class will have a significantly higher chance of achieving success as it relates to class and status than students that get an A in my cousins' math class in the city."

Anastasia Parker, please come to the principal's office. Anastasia Parker, please come to the principal's office.

The request came over the loudspeakers. The bell rang as Ana got up to leave. Her classmates slapped her on the back and a couple of them gave her a thumbs-up. This must be what it felt like to be Gwen, Ana mused. She was obviously receiving extra attention from her classmates for besting Mr. Little on a regular basis in a battle of wits. This was unfair, Ana thought. Mr. Little did not have much to work with.

"Ms. Boggs? I was told to come to the principal's office?" Ms. Boggs was a large older woman. Her perpetually red face got redder at the sight of Ana. She pursed her lips and adjusted her beehive hairdo. The office was busy with students coming in and out, but Ms. Boggs only looked at Ana.

"Ms. Boggs?" Ana repeated.

"Oh, yes. Sorry, dear. Please have a seat, Anastasia," Ms. Boggs replied, jumping up and spilling her coffee.

Ana took a seat. Ten minutes later, after the traffic inside had died down, the phones had stopped ringing, and Ms. Boggs had cleaned up her coffee, she faced Ana. "Sorry for the wait, Anastasia. What can I help you with?"

"I was called to the principal's office."

"Right, right, of course you were, dearie. But I don't think Dr. Gupta is in." Ms. Boggs looked carefully around the office, before walking to the principal's office. "Let me check. By the way, you haven't talked to your sister Gwen, have you?"

"No. Not since lunch. Why?"

"No reason. No reason. Just wondering. OK? Please don't mention anything to Gwen, OK?" Ms. Boggs said, wringing her hands. She practically had tears in her eyes. "Dr. Gupta? Dr. Gupta?" She knocked on his door. After a few seconds with no response, she added, "You know, let me check his calendar... Sorry, Anastasia. Dr. Gupta actually left earlier today. Silly me for forgetting. But I heard your name and it had to come from inside the office. You don't think Gwen could have... Oh, never mind, dearie. Never mind." Ms. Boggs rushed Ana out of the office and locked the door.

"OK. Thanks, Ms. Boggs," Ana managed to say before the door closed. *Gwen's shenanigans really have this administration wound too tight,* Ana thought.

School was out and the hallways were empty. Ana enjoyed the quiet. The two weeks since the park incident had been hectic for her. Gwen and Eve now scoured the Internet every day for fight moves they wanted to learn, and they expected Ana to teach them. Combined with Gwen's weight training and sparring sessions, Ana had barely enough time for reconnaissance, research, and her own business interests.

Ana heard the janitor behind her when she reached her locker. *Finally!* She thought. Turning around, she maced the janitor.

"Ah! My eyes!" He shouted, as he blindly reached for her. Ana ducked to the side. She hit him in the neck with her stun gun. He shook uncontrollably then collapsed. His clothes started smoking.

Ana hoped he was not hurt too bad. She knew he was genetically enhanced. He had to be. No ordinary person could take Gwen's punches like he had and survive, let alone recover so quickly. Ana had upped the wattage in her stun gun to ensure it would take him out. She kicked his mop cart out the way—the mop cart he had intended to stuff her in, Ana assumed. Rifling through his pockets, she grabbed his wallet. Her phone started playing music.

We're no strangers to love,
You know the rules and so do I...

"Hi Dad! Oh, you are outside right now? Sure, I'm on my way. I was just going over some extra math problems with Mr. Little... OK, see you in a sec. Bye! Eww!"

Ana jumped back. A puddle was growing under Lurch. *Hmm. Maybe my wattage is too high?* Ana thought.

Ana took all the money in his wallet, leaving it empty except for one bank deposit slip. Memorizing the account number on the slip, Ana dropped the wallet. Bending down, she placed a small transparent piece of plastic on his boot and beneath his collar. Briskly walking away, she counted the money. Twenty-seven dollars! She should go back and taser him again! How could a hired mercenary carry only twenty-seven dollars? Ana slowed her breathing, realizing it was not the janitor's fault.

This was obviously a direct result of corporations' Pyrrhic pursuit of higher profits at the expense of an ever-shrinking middle class. What was an honest mercenary to do? Ana just hoped he had health benefits.

"Hello, Mr. Little." Mr. Little was at his desk when Ana arrived in the classroom. Ana's locker was at the south end of the school with no exits. The only way out was probably being watched by Mr. Indubitably. She crossed the room as Mr. Little stared with his mouth open. She opened up the set of double windows and climbed out, and then walked around the building to the front entrance. She saw her dad waiting, with Eve and Gwen already in the car. Mr. Willis, the security guard, came running outside as she climbed in. Ana waved goodbye to him. He did not look pleased. Looking at him fume as they drove off, Ana wondered how much money he had in his wallet.

***

"Girls, your father has something he would like to tell you." Michelle directed her daughters to the couch.

Barry stood quietly until the girls were seated. He hated this. Hated it more than anything, but it was his comeuppance. "Girls... I, I'm... First, I would like to apologize for everything you've been through this year. More has been asked of you than is fair. Than is right."

"Dad... I would like to apologize. I'm sorry for—"

"No, Eve. You were right. It's not your fault. It's my fault. You're my daughters. It's my responsibility to protect you. I haven't done that. As a matter of fact I've done the opposite. I've put you at risk." Barry didn't think he would ever be able to look his daughters in the eye again. He had failed them. Utterly and completely failed them.

"Dad, we still don't know what you're talking about," Gwen said

"The way you are. What's happened to you; I... I did this to you."

"Father... can you clarify?"

"I can try, Ana..." He paused. "Before you were born I did something to myself that was selfish and stupid. And as a result you are the way you are. As a result you can't play basketball, run track, or do Tae Kwon Do. It's my fault that Robert and Melissa got hurt. It's my fault what happened to Mr. Newman. To Dr. Weaver."

"Did you take some type of drug?" Ana pressed.

"No. I had an operation."

"So you went to a hospital and had this operation?"

"That's not important right now, Ana. But I would like you to know that there is a cure. That we've found a cure."

Eve sat up. "A cure?"

"Yes. I have a friend. Who, for the last few months, has been searching for an antidote. I got word yesterday that he has it. He'll be here in a couple of weeks." It had come to this. Begging and threatening Dave to save his daughters. Humiliating.

"So he told you this over the phone?" Gwen asked, folding her arms and tilting her head.

"No. With everything that was going on, I didn't feel comfortable using a phone or email. So we used Fantasy Basketball."

"Fantasy Basketball?" Gwen scowled.

"Yeah. In college we made up a coded messaging system using Fantasy Basketball. The trick is finding a player with the right average

185

minutes played and free throw percentage. When we want to send a message we initiate a trade."

"That is actually quite brilliant in its simplicity!" Ana exclaimed

"Yeah. We thought we were pretty smart back then. We were pretty full of ourselves."

"But everything is going to be OK. You are going to be cured! You are going to be fine!" Michelle clutched her hands against her chest.

***

"The fox is in the hen house. The fox is in the henhouse and the cow jumped over the moon."

"Gwen, stop playing! This is serious," Eve replied back in her earpiece.

"Roger that, Roger," Gwen replied.

"Eve, me and Gwen have a visual on Lurch. Stick to the plan."

"OK. I think he's still behind me. I'm headed to the auditorium now." The school auditorium and the gym were on the lower level. Eve slowed her walk until the hall was empty. She then opened the door to the auditorium and entered. Once inside, she walked to the center of the stage and waited.

Seconds later the door slowly opened and shut.

Mr. Willis gave a dramatic flourish. "Ah! Eve! I'm so sorry it's come to this!"

"Me too," Eve responded.

"Alpha, Niner, Zero, Echo. The Eagle has landed and dad hates okra. Lurch wouldn't fit in the mop cart. We had to improvise. Our ETA is ten seconds. Mary had a little lamb. Alpha, Niner, Zero, Echo out. I mean, Roger that. No, I did mean out. Never mind. We're here," Eve heard in her earpiece. She could kill Gwen.

"Like I said, Eve, this should have been easy. You have put me in the unpromising position of engineering a child."

"It's uncompromising and endangering! My God, you are bad at this!" Gwen shouted from behind Mr. Willis.

Mr. Willis wheeled around. "You, you two are supposed to be in class!"

"Nurse pass." Gwen held up a piece of paper. "I have a headache."

Ana help up a similar piece of paper. "Me, too."

"Uh, well, I guess I find myself in this... an uneven position. But I expect my fortunes will be changing any second." Mr. Willis said, sweating and trying to smile.

"Lurch is duct-taped to a toilet. And it's unenviable," Gwen instructed, popping him in the back of his head.

"Well, I, just... well, if I may..."

"Shut up. I told you what would happen, didn't I?" Eve narrowed her eyes and lowered her voice.

"Well, let me..."

"That was a rhetorical question." Gwen popped him in the back of the head again and pressed down on his shoulders forcing him to his knees.

Eve walked forward. "If you want to live, tell us who your boss is."

"I can't. He'll kill me!"

"I'll kill you."

"You don't understand. He's crazy!"

"So you are refusing to cooperate?"

While Eve talked, Ana snatched his phone off his belt and grabbed his wallet from his back pocket. She handed the wallet to Eve. Taking out her computer from her backpack she plugged in his phone. Numbers scrolled up her screen. "We're good."

"Looks like we don't need your help. Ana knows who your boss is. Or at least, where he is. So you can tell him he can expect a visit from us."

"But… but…that's not possible."

"Not possible for me or you. But Ana's a genius, remember?" Eve took the phone from Ana and tossed it back to Mr. Willis, along with his wallet.

"Wait…" Ana turned to Mr. Willis. "Mr. Willis, may I please have your wallet?"

Mr. Willis carefully handed his wallet to Ana.

"Thank you, Mr. Willis." Ana took all the money out. "Now, would you mind turning your pockets inside out?"

Mr. Willis looked to Eve for help. Eve ignored him. He emptied his pockets. A large money clip fell to the floor. Ana handed Mr. Willis back his wallet and retrieved the money clip.

Eve was irritated by this. "What are you doing?"

"Monies derived through illegal activity are subject to forfeiture."

"Ana, I don't like this."

"Eve, this… seven hundred and ninety-seven dollars was secured by Mr. Willis illegally. Undoubtedly to watch and then capture us. And I have absolutely no qualms relieving an inept kidnapper of his ill-gotten gains."

Eve glared at Ana, her hands on her hips.

Ana squared off against Eve and matched her glare without flinching. "I am not under any circumstances going to give Mr. Willis this money back."

"You get a pass this time. But understand this; if it happens again, you and I are going to have a problem."

"I'm with Eve. Superheroes don't roll like this. You're breakin bad, Ana, and it's not cool."

***

"How did you know Mr. Willis would come after me? You said Lurch came after you at school because you made yourself available, and they considered you the weakest link. But why me?"

"Simple. You are always alone. Gwen is always surrounded by friends."

"Wow! Way to be subtle, Band Geek!"

"She asked."

"So where are we with finding out who they work for?" Eve continued. Ana's logic was sound; it would make more sense to target a loner. There was no need to get worked up over it.

"We?"

"Ana, you know what I mean."

"Well, 'we' are having problems with 'our' bugs flickering in and out. But as far as 'we' can tell, both Lurch and Mr. Willis's daily patterns haven't changed. Also Mr. Willis's old phone never made any outgoing calls. It received one incoming a couple of days ago from a burner that was purchased in Washington DC, and he has a new phone now. Whoever they work for, they are good at covering their tracks."

Gwen leaned in closer to Ana. "What do you mean flickering in and out?"

"The bugs use cell phone signals. I don't track where Mr. Willis and Lurch are. I track the cell phone or phones that are closest to them. The rundown hotel they are staying at does not have a lot of cell phone users in close proximity."

Gwen look confused. "Why not use a regular bug like on TV?"

"Because they're garish and easily discovered. Mine are much more elegant and biodegradable," Ana stated proudly.

"But the plan was for him to panic and contact his boss. Sounds like that didn't happen, at least not in a way that we have identified. So how is your plan to secure an antidote or cure coming?" The fact that they could not discern whether Lurch or Mr. Willis had attempted to contact anyone was troubling to Eve. She had willingly put herself at risk and they had nothing to show for it.

"Slowly. I'm waiting to see if Dad's friend can deliver."

"I hate to interrupt you two geniuses, but that's a trap."

"What are you talking about, Gwen? What's a trap?"

"Jeez, Princess! You need to put down the books and watch more TV. Someone has been one step ahead of us, right? At the hospital?

190

At the pharmacy building? Remember that cable van we saw the beginning of the school year? Remember those two scary police officers? Whoever was in that van probably bugged our house and was probably working with those two police officers, if they didn't do it themselves."

"How do you know?"

"I don't, Ana. Not for sure anyway. But I bet if you stopped robbing people for a few days you could probably find bugs in our house. And hey, I thought you said that David was off the grid? No electronic footprint? Remember that?"

"David must be using his school's email address from his college days. And to be honest, checking Fantasy Basketball for coded messages didn't cross my mind. Nevertheless, you have a point about the house and bugs. I'll get right on it."

"So what makes you think Dad's friend is setting a trap?"

"Are you listening, Princess? Dad's friend isn't. Whoever those supercops work for is. Dad told us in our bugged house. They now know everything we know."

Eve was getting frustrated. None of this made sense to her. "But what about Mr. Willis and Lurch? If they know everything, how come they're still after us? Aren't they with the fake cops?"

"Yeah, right! Mr. Willis and Lurch are clowns. There is absolutely no way they're working with those fake supercops. Those fake police are the real deal. They're professional and at the top of their game."

Ana looked at Gwen and crossed her arms. "And you know all this because?"

"Because I have a sixth sense about these things."

"Not good enough, Gwen. I'm with Ana on this. How do you know all this?"

"OK, OK. It just makes sense. Think about it. They took all the drugs out the hospital so we couldn't get 'em. It's like they wanted us to go to that pharmacy building. It's what I would have done. And why haven't those supercops made a move? It's because they're just biding their time, gathering information. They plan on catching us, Dad's friend, and the antidote together. That's what I would do, anyway."

"But that doesn't explain how you know Mr. Willis and Lurch are not with the fake police?" Ana persisted.

"Seriously? For someone who's supposed to be a genius you're about as dumb as a box of rocks, sometimes. And what about you, Princess? They don't cover this stuff in Jane Austen novels? Just think about it... can you imagine Mr. Indubitably and Lurch being hired by the same person that vetted and hired those cops? Yeah, me neither."

"First, don't ever use Jane Austen and Mr. Indubitably in the same sentence again. Second, if you know all this, how come you're just now mentioning it?"

"I don't know it! I'm not sure about any of it! It just makes sense to me. And what are you getting so mad about? You and Ana are supposed to me the smart ones!"

Eve had to give Gwen the benefit of the doubt. After they'd mulled it over for a few minutes, her theory didn't seem so farfetched. "So, what do we do now?"

"Easy. Walk into the trap," Gwen replied.

"Excuse me? I know I'm dumb as a box of rocks, but isn't walking into a trap counterproductive?"

"Super Dork, you're missing the point! It's no longer a trap. At least not for us, anyway."

"So are you saying we set a counter-trap? Catch them instead of them catching us?"

"Please, Princess! What would we do with them after we catch 'em? We can't even get a dog, you think Mom and Dad are going to let us have a hostage? And who would clean up after 'em and feed 'em? You can count me out."

"OK, smarty-pants. What do we do?"

"Depends on what we want, right? And what we want is to be left alone. We need leverage for that."

"Leverage? What is this leverage you speak of, and how do we acquire it?"

"Boy, you guys really need to watch more TV. We get leverage by finding out who the top dog is!"

Eve breathed in deeply. No matter how hard they tried, they kept tumbling deeper down the rabbit hole. She looked directly at Gwen. "Are you confident we can do this?"

"No, I'm not. But what choice do we have?"

Chapter 14

Gwen tried to ignore Rebecca, who kept looking at her in an attempt to get her attention.

"So, Gwen—have you heard from Elizabeth?" Rebecca eventually blurted.

"Rebecca, you ask that every day. And every day I say no. Can we please stop talking about it now?"

"I'm sorry. It's just that, you know... No one has heard from her since you and Eve put her dad in the hospital." The table went quiet. Everyone looked at Gwen. For once, Gwen was at a loss for words. So much had happened lately that the Mr. Newman incident seemed like years ago to Gwen. But it was all the school talked about.

"Hey, on the news last night they said that the Aborigine rugby team is part of some international drug smuggling cartel. They traced them all the way back to Australia," Toni said, breaking the tension at the table.

"I saw that!" Rebecca exclaimed. "The FBI has been after them for years!"

This elicited a laugh from Gwen. Tracking the crazy rugby team had taken on a life of its own in their sleepy little suburb. The press conferences that the chief of police gave in his vow to bring the international cartel to justice were some of the funniest things she had ever seen. But her laughter was brief. She had been right about their house being bugged. It had taken Ana a week to find them all. Also, Gwen knew she was on borrowed time. Dave was supposed to have contacted them two weeks ago. Nada. Anxious to do something to occupy her mind, Gwen blurted, "Hey, Eric, is what I heard true? Did Jeff and Tom try to stuff you in a locker?"

Eric spoke softly while looking down. "Yes, milady." Eric was a gamer. A few gamers, skaters, artists, and social stragglers always sat at Gwen's table. It was commonly referred to as the table of misfit students. Gwen was proud of the moniker, which had started last year after Gwen knocked down two girls for bullying Emily. The following week, Emily and her friends started sitting with Gwen. Not long after that, they started providing items of food and speaking to Gwen in archaic English. It was a running joke that wasn't funny and, as Eve constantly reminded her, had been running too long.

"Eric, Emily, grab a tray and come with me." Gwen stood up. Rebecca and Dana stood as well, but Gwen shook her head, motioning for them to sit down, which they reluctantly did.

"Girl, don't do anything crazy," Toni said, as Gwen sauntered off to the jock table with Eric and Emily in tow.

Gwen watched the teachers' table out of the corner of her eye. Ms. Boggs spoke into a walkie-talkie with wide eyes. She attempted to stand, but Mrs. Adams grabbed her by the arm and guided her back down.

"Hey, boys! How's it going?" Gwen asked, interrupting the conversation. She stopped directly behind Jeff and Tom.

"Hey, Peppermint Patty! Watch your step!" laughed Jeff, along with the rest of the table, but no one more loudly then Javier.

"Jeffy! You got jokes? You funny? I didn't know you were funny, Jeffy!" Gwen reached over Jeff, grabbed his pizza, and shoved it in her mouth.

"Karate Kid, could you please run along? Or better yet, run and tell your sister that I want her to call me. Tyler didn't know what to do with that anyway!" The table laughed louder.

Gwen held up a finger for silence while she finished chewing. "Jeffy! You a ladies' man too? A ladies' man *and* funny?" She put a hand on Jeff's shoulder, slowly squeezing it. Jeff's demeanor changed from hilarity to discomfort, to pain. He tried to stand up. Gwen roughly sat him back down. The laughter stopped.

"No, Jeffy… I'm here because we have a failure to communicate." Gwen was still smiling. "My friend Emily, here… say hi, Emily."

"Hullo."

"Thanks… Anyway, Emily told me something I am having a hard time believing… Jeffy? Jeffy? Did you hear me? You don't look so good, Jeffy. If you understand what I am saying, please nod."

Jeff nodded rapidly. Beads of sweat formed on his forehead. Tom stood up. Gwen grabbed him by the back of his neck with her other hand, and forcibly sat him back down.

"Tommy! Where you going? Do you need to go to the little boys' room or something? Don't worry, Tommy, I'll just be a minute... Hey Tommy, were you going to eat the rest of that pizza?"

Tommy shook his head, grimacing.

"Great! Hey Eric, can you grab Tommy's pizza for me? You know what, grab that apple too, and don't forget his cake. Thanks… Oh now, Tommy, did you hear what I was saying to everyone's favorite funny guy and ladies' man?" Gwen started squeezing his neck.

"Gwen, that hurts! Let me go!" Tom struggled to rise. His voice drew stares from other students in the cafeteria. Gwen looked around casually. Mrs. Boggs pulled out her walkie-talkie again, but Mrs. Adams put her hand over it. The teachers were watching intently.

"Whoa! Tommy! Turn it down a notch, tiger! All this attention is making me blush! But if you keep raising your voice like that I might take it the wrong way. I might have to squeeze a little harder. Tommy? Are you still with me? If so, just nod…"

Tom nodded.

"Great! Oh, and see my friend Eric here. Say hi, Eric."

"Hullo."

"Thanks, Eric… So anyway, Emily says that you two pillars of the community and model students attempted to stuff Eric in a locker! But I know that can't be true because I issued an… a… what was it again, Eric?"

"An edict, milady."

"Yeah, I issued an edict that said, um… oh, I forgot again. What did my edict say, Eric?"

"Henceforth, any able-bodied man or woman that sweareth fealty to Lady Gwen shall not be subject to provocation."

"Don't you just love it when he talks like that? So anyway, I issued my edict basically saying no one messes with my friends who sit with me at my table. Are you two studs still with me?"

Tom and Jeff nodded desperately, while grimacing and sweating. The table of ten of the most popular and physically imposing male athletes in the school watched in silence.

"And you two tough guys violated that edict. And you know what bothers me the most about it? Look at Eric. He is not that big at all. It would not be very challenging to stuff him in a locker. And are we not at this fine institution to challenge ourselves?"

"We're sorry, Gwen," Jeff whispered, dripping sweat.

"Oh, I know you're sorry, Jeffy. Football team only had three wins this season, right? Thank God for the girls' basketball team, right? Hey, Jeffy, you're a strapping young lad. What do you go for, about one-ninety?"

"One eighty-five," Jeff whispered.

"And you, Tommy?"

"One ninety-seven," Tommy cried out.

"Whoa! Tommy you got some junk in the trunk! I bet stuffing you in a locker would be a real challenge! Who's with me?"

Javier glared at her. "Let them go, Gwen."

She matched Javier's stare. She squeezed both hands tighter; both boys squealed in pain, drawing gasps from the table. Gwen released her grip. She started talking and walking around the table. "Boys, I'm going to need your help." She pointed at food, indiscriminately. Eric and Emily put the food on their tray without interference.

"I promised my folks that I would not do anything crazy this year. But my dad is old-fashioned. He might categorize stuffing football players in lockers as crazy. I know, I know, but he's my dad, so what are you going to do, right? So anyway, could you please be nice to my friends? Because if you guys ruin my chances of getting drums this summer I will be very angry. And you boys would not like me when I'm angry."

Eric nodded at the football players, who were seething. "Gwen, let's just go."

Gwen looked briefly at Eric and nodded. "Jeffy boy, you are hilarious! 'Pepper-mint Patty!' 'Karate Kid!' Dude, you crack me up. And Javier, all your hair is back. You looking good, papi! You should call me." Grabbing an apple off of Javier's plate, Gwen devoured it loudly in three large bites. "And with that, gentlemen, I bid you adieu." She set the core back down on Javier's tray and wiped her mouth with his napkin.

Eric kept his distance from Gwen on the way back to the table. When she looked at him, he quickly turned away. But Gwen saw the way he'd looked at her. It resembled the look of the police and her neighbors the day she hurt Mr. Newman. Sort of how a person might look at a freak.

Sitting down at the table, Gwen pretended to enjoy herself. Toni shattered her façade by saying, "Gwen your nose is bleeding!"

***

Two weeks until the end of school. Mr. Willis and Lurch were still at the school but gave the Parker sisters a wide berth. David never showed or contacted them. For Eve, headaches and nosebleeds were happening every week now; she had successfully hidden them from her parents but, with their increased frequency, chances were slim she could keep that up.

Tyler and Eve were still not talking. Eve wanted to apologize. She wanted to hold his hand and have him smile at her with those irresistible dimples. But most of all she wanted to make peace with him, and tell him how much he meant to her. Unfortunately, Tyler was never alone and Eve doubted she had the nerve to approach him even if he was.

Closing her locker, Eve headed for the gym. The other students keep their distance as she passed. Since her fight with Tyler, she had become persona non grata. But the students were smart enough not to get in her face. No one ever confronted her and gossip was kept at a minimum when she was around. Which was fine with Eve.

"OK everyone, calm down! Calm down! School's not over yet!" Mrs. Wynn yelled to her restless charges. "John, keep your hands to yourself!" Mrs. Wynn said to Big John, as he pushed a smaller boy out the way.

Big John, the largest kid in school by far, by width if not height, towered over the other boys. He stood over six feet with light brown curly hair and freckles. His stomach peeked out the bottom of his gym shirt as he scowled at Mrs. Wynn, while he flexed his muscular arms.

"Coach! Coach! Can we play dodge ball! Girls against boys!" Lucia shouted.

Before she acknowledged her star pitcher, Mrs. Wynn eyed Big John until he looked away. A tall, slender woman, Mrs. Wynn had a commanding presence and students seldom openly challenged her. The entire school respected her, as her volleyball and softball teams were two of the only sports teams that consistently had winning seasons. "OK. Dodge ball it is. Girls against boys!" She smiled. The gym cheered her decision, but Mrs. Wynn never said no to her star pitcher.

"Hey, Lucia. Congratulations on being valedictorian," Eve said, while walking with Lucia. Ms. Grant had pulled her, Amy, and Lucia aside a couple of days ago and told them the news. Missing so much school had finally caught up with Eve. But she'd always liked and admired Lucia, and she was genuinely happy for her. Although not a small girl, Lucia carried herself with a sense of pride, and her constant upbeat attitude was infectious.

"Thanks, Eve!" Lucia replied, as they made their way to the other side of the gym where the girls were congregating.

"Hey, Eve," Amy said, joining them.

"Hey, Amy." Amy and Eve had reverted to being cordial toward each other without being friendly. Like everyone else in school, Amy had given Eve the cold shoulder over her breakup with Tyler.

As the girls gathered at one end of the gym, Eve lifted her grey gym shirt over her stomach. She tied a knot in the back to secure it. The move displayed her six-pack abs to everyone present. Gwen was a taskmaster but her workouts got results. Eve's legs were still big, but they were also visibly more muscular beneath her blue gym shorts. She rolled up the sleeves of her T-shirt over her shoulders. Though not as big as Gwen's her arms were still impressive, with more definition than anyone else's in class, boys included. She wanted everyone to witness the results of her countless hours of sparring and working out.

Her classmates gaped. Eve imagined the image she presented: Dark-skinned, muscular, afro exploding out the back of her head wrap. *It's a new day!* Eve smiled to herself. She didn't know how long she had, but it didn't matter. Every day was a blessing and it was time to live like there was no tomorrow. Because in her case there might not be. With a slight smile, she stood with hands on hips, pretending not to notice the stares.

"OK, OK, everyone line up!" Coach Wynn shouted.

The game started with a row of balls in the middle of the gym. The two teams faced each other, each participant with a hand on the wall.

Amy nodded to Eve. They smiled at each other. *This is going to be fun!* Eve thought.

The whistle blew. There was a mad dash to the balls. Eve got there first, followed by Amy. They both pushed as many balls as they could back to their teammates. The girls ended up with seven balls, while the boys had three.

Flanked on both sides by Amy and Lucia, Eve advanced to the center of the gym with a ball. She smiled at the boys, who looked tentative. After being egged on by their teammates, all three threw at Eve, who easily dodged the only ball that was on target. She, Amy, and Lucia unloaded on the retreating boys; all three girls found their targets. But Lucia made a statement— the impact of her ball could be heard throughout the gym. Her target walked off slowly, forcing a smile. The girls taunted him as he took a seat next to the other two boys.

Big John grabbed a ball. Running forward he fired it, catching Lucia in the face. He ran backward, laughing and pointing at Lucia. Lucia looked stunned.

Amy rushed over to her.

"Lucia! Are you OK?" The action stopped. Lucia waved Amy away; she gave a theatrical bow and strutted to the sideline, to a chorus of cheers from the girls.

The other girls hastily launched their balls in retaliation. Three balls were easily caught. John hit another girl on her side as she ran for cover. She gingerly walked to the side to join her teammates. Four girls were left, including Amy and Eve. Amy grabbed the ball that had hit Lucia. Two boys missed Eve by a wide margin as two other boys connected with their targets. Just Amy and Eve were left. Amy hurled her ball directly at Big John's head. He barely managed to block it with his ball. It ricocheted high into the air. Another boy caught it. Amy cut her eyes at John as she walked off.

It was Eve against Big John and three other boys. The gym started reverberating with the noise of Amy, Lucia, and the rest of the girls cheering her on. Eve smiled. She'd missed this.

The boys advanced. Each of them had a ball; two boys threw together, and Eve caught one. Throwing it down, she dived and caught the second. Both throwers were out. Rolling to her feet she blocked a ball aimed at her head. She almost laughed—Big John was nothing if not predictable. He cursed as he backpedaled. The last boy threw his ball. Running forward, Eve caught the weak thrown ball off a bounce and still running, she threw it, catching her victim between the shoulder blades as he turned to run. The girls were ecstatic.

This feels good! Eve thought, as she paused to bask in the moment. The gym was reverberating with shouts and screams.

Only John was left. Closing her eyes for a second Eve visualized her plan. Walking backward she bent down to pick up two balls. Big John stayed back as Eve walked to the center. Taking a quick step she threw at John underhand. The style was similar to Lucia's but unlike Lucia, Eve's throw had no velocity—her ball soared high into the air. Throwing his ball down Big John ran to catch it, gloating.

Eve watched. Before John caught the ball Eve switched her second ball to her right hand. Taking a quick step forward, she put everything she had into her throw—the ball left her hand like a rocket. Big John froze. His indecision cost him. Eve's second ball went through his hands and hit him between the eyes. Her first thrown ball simultaneously bounced off the top of his head. The gym went crazy; Eve was mobbed. Amy was there first, bear-hugging her. Even the boys were cheering.

"Settle down! Settle down! OK, you know the rules. The losing team gets the balls. Everyone else hit the showers!" Coach Wynn walked to her office, smiling and shaking her head.

"Eve, I wish you could have played ball this year!" Lucia was hugging Eve with one arm. "We could have gone all the way!"

"Leave me alone!" A boy yelled behind them.

The girls turned around. Big John shoved a boy down as he tried to stand up. Another boy was already on the ground looking around for help. Nobody helped. Eve knew the boys; they were in her honors math class. They were skinny, pale, and together were no match for Big John. The taller one—Andrew—had acne, and looked terrified.

"Stop it, John!" yelled Amy, as she went to help.

"Mind your own business, Amy! I'm just having a little fun with my friends," replied Big John, as he shoved another one of the boys down.

Amy helped a boy up. The other boy quickly ran behind her. "What is wrong with you, John? Why can't you just leave people alone?"

"I told you to mind your own business!"

"John, you are a bully and a punk. Why don't you just grow up?" Amy poked John in the chest while she spoke.

John pushed her hand roughly to the side. "Little girl, you need to get out of my face before something bad happens to you."

"No! I'm sick and tired of you!" Amy shouted. She tried to push John away with both hands. He didn't budge. Lucia was at her side now; she attempted to pull Amy away, but Amy yanked her arm back.

"Leave! Just go!" Amy yelled at John. She pushed harder. He took a half step back.

Big John puffed out his chest. He punched Amy with open palms in both of her shoulders; she stumbled back and went down hard. Lucia, who tried to catch her, went down with her. One of the boys ran to the teacher's office.

"Thanks for not inviting me to your lame birthday party!" John stood over Amy and Lucia and gave everyone in the gym a threatening look, warning them with his eyes to stay back.

Eve ignored the look. "John, you better leave now," she said, inserting herself between him and Amy.

"Get out of my face, Eve! This is between me and Amy!" Taking a step back, John attempted to push Eve down. Without thinking, Eve did a front snap kick to his stomach. She followed that with a spinning back kick to the same spot. The kick landed flush. Eve felt the air leave his body. She finished with a roundhouse to the side of his face. The kick made a loud clapping sound when it connected, echoing through the gym. The force of the kick sent John stumbling sideways. He then dropped to one knee, holding his stomach.

The students were speechless.

Eve took a couple of deep breaths. She saw Mrs. Wynn running toward them. John was still on one knee; leaning on one arm for balance, he glared at Eve.

Eve took note of John's glare while gauging the distance between them. She thought of the way Big John always looked at her. Looks intended to make her feel like an object. Looks intended to put her in her place. She also knew that John told everyone her grandmother made her fortune by shaking down companies. First, Eve would not be objectified by anyone. Second, her grandmother was a civil rights icon and a national treasure. Eve started bouncing on her toes.

"Stop it! Stop it! Eve, don't!" Coach Wynn yelled. She was only a few feet away, but Eve was not stopping. This is what her grandmother would call a teachable moment. Taking one step she blasted in the air. She hit Big John across his jaw with a flying knee. He did a full turn, landing on his back, his arms extended like he was making snow angels.

He was unconscious. Eve landed on her hands and knees. Sitting up, she felt confident her knee had taught John to be more mindful of his eyes and tongue.

Lucia and Amy helped Eve to her feet.

"John! John!" Mrs. Wynn yelled. She was kneeling down next to John. Every time she said his name, she clapped her hands in front of his face. Disoriented, he slowly opened his eyes. The gym started talking again. The two boys who'd been bullied by John started speaking rapidly to Mrs. Wynn.

"I got it! I got it! Everyone hit the showers. Now!" Mrs. Wynn waved her hand, dismissing the class. "You three! In my office!" She pointed at Amy, Lucia, and Eve while helping John to his feet.

Once inside coach Wynn's office Lucia would not stop talking. "Eve, oh my God! That was incredible! Did you learn that at Kang's school?"

"Yes," Eve answered, but there was nothing incredible about her performance. No super-speed. No flash of heat; nothing incredible at all. Eve found that troubling.

"Do Kang's parents have any schools in the city? Do you know how much classes are? Does Kang teach any classes? That jumping knee thing or whatever was like something out of a movie! I have to learn it. You dropped him like it was nothing!" Lucia continued.

Amy and Eve remained quiet.

The girls sat in three chairs opposite Mrs. Wynn's desk, with Eve in the middle.

"Hey, girls." Mrs. Wynn came in closing the door behind her. "Lucia, how is your face? That was a pretty vicious shot you took from John."

"I'm OK, coach. It hurt a little at first, but not so much now."

"So you don't have any reservations about playing tonight? Shoulder feeling good? Ready to pitch another no-hitter? This is a big game for us. I would hate not to have you."

"Coach, I'm fine! Besides, there's no way I would miss the game!"

"Great. Glad to hear… Amy, how are you feeling?"

"OK. Butt is a little sore."

"Not too sore to miss your track meet, I hope? You've been having an excellent season."

"Thanks. I'm sure I'll be OK."

"And Eve, what is going on with you and your sisters? What is this strange ailment that prevents you from participating in sports?"

"I'm not quite sure what it is. We've been trying to schedule an examination with a specialist. But he has been tough to pin down." Eve was surprised by Mrs. Wynn's demeanor. Two minutes ago, she had acted like the girls were in real trouble. Now she was acting like nothing happened.

"Well, I wish you and your sisters the best. It just breaks my heart that someone with your gifts cannot compete. Keep focusing on your studies and I'm sure everything will work out for the best."

"Thanks, Mrs. Wynn. I will."

"Good. And once you get the OK to compete again you should seriously consider softball. With your speed and athleticism you'd be great. You would need to take your time and learn the fundamentals, of course."

"Yes, Eve, think about softball. You would do great! And I would be more than happy to work with you!" Lucia added, cheerfully.

Amy and Eve exchanged looks, and Amy asked, "Mrs. Wynn, what about John?"

Mrs. Wynn laughed, while handing each girl a late pass. "Don't worry about John. He says he can't remember anything. The little bit I saw I imagine that's not true. He just doesn't want to remember anything... OK, girls! Off you go!"

"Eve, you should come to my party this weekend," Lucia said, as they headed for their next class.

"Yeah, Eve. It's going to be cool. And you'll love Lucia's grandmother. But brush up on your Spanish because her English is not that good. But she is so funny!"

"I'll have to ask my parents. Where is it and what is it your birthday party?"

"No. It's sorta like a block party—" Lucia started, before she was interrupted by Amy.

"What Lucia is trying to say is that everyone in her neighborhood is so proud of her for being valedictorian and beating all the rich kids, that they're throwing her a party." Amy teased, as she playfully hip bumped Lucia.

"Really?"

"Well. I guess. But you know, I get to do most of my studying on the train. So it's not really that big of a deal."

"I think it's great," Eve replied, before stopping and leaning against a wall.

Amy grabbed Eve by the shoulder. "Eve?"

"Eve! Oh my God! Something is coming out of your ear!" Eve heard Lucia yell, before she lost consciousness.

***

"Mr. and Mrs. Parker? How did you get here so fast? As I said over the phone, Eve experienced a dizzy spell and fainted. This was probably related to an altercation she'd had with another student. She appears to be OK now, but her temperature's a little low, so if I were you I would definitely take her in."

"Thanks, Mrs. Brock. We were actually on our way to pick up the girls anyway. How low is her temperature?"

"Ninety-six degrees."

"Eve? Let's go, hon." Michelle wrapped her arm around Eve and helped her stand, while Barry signed the girls out.

"Mom, I'm OK. I was just dizzy for a minute. I'm fine now," Eve lied, as she pulled away. Her headache made it hard to focus and she couldn't remember the last time she'd felt this cold. Using her best acting skills she smiled and walked to the car.

Gwen and Ana were waiting beside it. Gwen stepped in front of Eve. "Everything OK, sis? Everyone is talking about what happened in gym."

"I'm OK. The John thing was just a case of mistaken identity. He didn't know who I was." Eve got in the car and closed her eyes. It was a warm, sunny day and it took everything Eve had to stop her teeth from chattering.

"Hey, Band Geek! Where you going? Get in the back!" Gwen pulled Ana back by her collar and rushed into the minivan ahead of her.

"I always ride in the back!" Ana complained, as she climbed past Gwen to the back. "And I'm in orchestra!"

Gwen ignored Ana. "So Dad, what's the deal? Your friend get back to you?"

"Yes. We're going to meet him right now."

"Can't we stop at home? I have to pick up something?"

"No! Gwen this is serious! We've been waiting for over a month for this. We're going straight to the city and getting this over with."

"The city? Father, would it not be more prudent to drop off our school supplies first?"

"No! No, Ana, it would not be more prudent. What is wrong with you girls? This is a big deal. And Dave is nervous about being followed or something. He's worried that if we can't get this done now it might be another six months before we can meet again."

Eve and Gwen looked at each other. Eve knew what she was thinking—they had planned for this meeting; they had prepared for this meeting. But they had become complacent after the date kept getting pushed further out. They didn't think it was going to happen; they'd stopped bringing everything they needed. They were going into a trap blind and unprepared.

211

Gwen continued. "So where are we going?"

"My old neighborhood."

"Can we go to the basketball court where you got beat up as a kid? Do you think that guy still lives there? I bet you can take him now, Dad."

"Gwen, I did not get beat up. It was just a scuffle if anything."

"Uncle Brian says you were thrashed rather thoroughly," Ana offered.

"When did you talk to your Uncle Brian? I thought he was, uh, still away traveling?"

"Father, if you mean incarcerated he has been out for two months. Antonio and Emmitt talk to him all the time."

"Girls, I am not comfortable with you speaking to your Uncle Brian without me or your mother being involved. We have had these discussions before."

"Is it because of the fake church and donations thing?" Gwen asked

"No, it must be because of the borrowing cars thing," Ana noted.

"The casting agent was the best one ever!" Gwen replied.

"Hardly. It paled in complexity and profit margin to the real estate investor," Ana countered.

"Please stop talking about your Uncle Brian," their mother announced, with a tone of finality.

Forty minutes later, they were driving around the neighborhood their father had grown up in. His old housing project had long been torn down, but nothing had been built to replace it. Eve didn't like what she

212

saw. This wasn't her first time in the area, but it was the first time she'd actually noticed the surroundings: the streets were abandoned; the buildings were boarded up; the sidewalks were in disrepair; and trash was everywhere. *The things I take for granted*, Eve thought, shaking her head.

Michelle looked at Eve through her rearview mirror. "Eve, are you feeling OK now?"

"Yes, Mom. I told you, I'm fine."

Barry turned around, smiling. "Eve, we're going to make you better. I promise."

"I know, Dad."

"OK, stop here. That's where we're supposed to meet." Barry pointed to a train underpass across the street that was littered with debris.

"Check it out! Some wannabe thugs." Gwen nodded at two boys leaning against an abandoned brick building. They were directly across the street from the meeting spot and diagonal to the Parkers' minivan. One boy appeared to be preoccupied reading a comic book. The other stared intently into the car. His body language and posture indicated this was his neighborhood.

Gwen blurted, "Dad, is that him?" while pointing to a man who was cautiously walking to the underpass while the two boys watched.

"Yes. You girls wait here while I go—"

"Dad, don't go! Look!" Gwen shouted.

"Why?"

"That homeless guy pushing the shopping cart. He's built like a linebacker." Gwen pointed to a man across the street from their car and diagonal to the meeting place.

"Gwen, it's OK. I grew up in this area. Trust me: homeless people come in all shapes and sizes."

"Dad, we should listen to Gwen," Eve added.

"Right! Dad, I'll go with you. Eve, you follow the homeless guy. Mom, get ready to come get me and Dad ASAP! Ana, stay with Mom and keep your eyes on everything. OK?" As she spoke, Gwen looked at her family members one at a time. Eve and Ana nodded in unison.

"No, Gwen. Not OK. You and Eve are not leaving this car."

"But Mom, Dad cannot go out there alone. And Eve is fast enough to do something if the homeless guy makes a move. Outside of Dad, you're the only one who can drive."

"No. No! You and Eve are not getting out of this car. End of discussion!"

"Girls, I agree with your mother. I'll be fine." He gave his wife a kiss and whispered, "It will be over soon, babe." He exited the car.

The boys across the street watched his every move.

Gwen climbed into the front seat. She scanned everything; Ana and Eve were just as vigilant. Eve's chills and headache had been replaced by anxiety and focus.

"There is someone on the roof!" Gwen shouted. She jumped out, racing toward her Father.

"Get back in the car! Now!" Michelle yelled, jumping out herself.

"Mom! Get back in the car! Keep an eye on Dad and Gwen! Ana, do not leave Mom!" Eve shouted, as she jumped out and raced across the street.

Eve hoped she was in the homeless man's blind spot as she closed in on him from behind. She was ten feet away when she realized Gwen was right. The homeless man had on a black vest obscured beneath his ragged clothing. Eve quickened her pace. Scanning the area she saw her father and Gwen were a few steps away from Dave. She didn't see the two boys.

The homeless man's body language changed. He stood upright and his whole frame looked tense. Eve quickened her pace again while attempting to watch everything; she saw her Father and Dave shake hands, and watched as Dave handed her father something. Then everything happened at once. She heard gunfire from the top of a building. Gwen knocked her father to the ground, covering him with her body. Dave turned and ran. Eve heard the squealing tires of their minivan. The homeless man turned around. He had a gun pointed directly at her.

Game time.

Eve had never been more ready. She kicked his gun hand. The gun fired a couple of inches above her head. She felt the bullet go by. Her adrenaline was pumping. She stepped into a reverse spinning kick. It landed on his throat. He stumbled back, gasped, and re-aimed his gun. Eve shadowed him.

As the gun swung toward her, she stepped in and ducked under his arm. She grabbed his gun hand, pulling it back toward her while simultaneously striking the back of his elbow with her forearm. She felt his elbow crack. Letting go of his hand, she struck upward with her palm. The cartilage in his nose collapsed; his nose spewed blood. She kicked him in the stomach, but her foot bounced of his vest. Grabbing his gun hand with both of hers, she twisted it so the gun was pointed at his chest. Something snapped. He dropped the gun. Eve jumped back, just avoiding the knife thrust from his other hand. But she couldn't move fast enough to dodge his kick, which caught her in the chest. She was weightless, then she landed hard. She was out of breath. He advanced. She saw his face for the first time. Except it wasn't the first time; he was one of the police officers who had come to the house.

"Get up, Eve! It's the fourth quarter, girl!" she shouted, spitting blood and scrambling to her feet.

His distorted arm hung useless at his side. The other had a knife. They both spotted the gun between them, and eyed each other as they circled it.

"*Come on!*" Eve screamed. The ferocity of her scream shocked her and gave her courage. Her adversary also paused, while tilting his head to observe her.

Eve kicked off her flats and hiked up her black slacks. She waited for the attack. He didn't advance.

I got this! Eve thought. She wiped her bleeding nose with the back of her hand and ripped off her pink blouse, all while never losing eye contact. Wrapping her blouse around both hands she judged the distance between them.

His bloody face displayed no emotion. It was just business to him. He carefully used his knife hand to toss off his homeless rags.

Eve set her feet. The sidewalk felt grimy on her bare feet. She slowly inched forward. He watched. They both stared unblinking. Eve was dialed in. She couldn't see anything else. She couldn't hear anything else. He shifted his weight. Eve attacked. She snared his knife hand with her blouse and both her hands. She kneed him twice in the groin. He shuddered, coughed blood, and took a step back. He attempted to wrench his hand free. *Perfect!* she thought. She didn't resist. His effort created space between them. Letting one hand go, she kicked him in the jaw; the impact jolted her entire body. It was like kicking Gwen. She kicked him again in the jaw. Her knee almost buckled.

Predictably, he kicked back. Stepping inside his kick, Eve uppercut him with her free hand. It was like punching a car—pain shot up her arm, and her hand went numb. He spit blood, kneed her in the stomach, and tried to wrench his knife hand free.

Don't let go! Eve thought, as she gasped for air. His knife hand was still tangled up in her blouse. If she let go she was dead. His jerking motion created the space Eve needed again. Her stomach cramping, she kicked him again in the jaw. Something cracked; she didn't know if it was his jaw or her foot. His eyes rolled to the back of his head. He stumbled. Eve exhaled. He blinked, shook his head, and regained his balance. Spitting blood, Eve launched into him. Kneeing him again in the groin, she tried to push his scrotum up into his chest cavity. She then hit him in the jaw with her elbow and she pushed back off with a kick to his chest. Pain shot up her leg; her foot was definitely broken. But something had moved when she hit him with her elbow—his jaw was broken as well.

"I. Am. Not. Dying. Today!" Eve shouted at him. She ignored the pain shooting up her leg; she ignored her broken hand. She willed herself to stand. Her opponent was laboring to breathe. He was coughing up blood, and blood was streaming from his nose; the left side of his face was red and starting to swell, and his eyes were watering. His left eye was half-closed. She was breaking him. He was angry now. Maybe scared, too. Legs shaking, heart pounding, Eve grimaced, kicking again with her broken foot. He stepped in, avoided her kick and head-butted her. For the second time that day, Eve lost consciousness.

***

"Eve! Eve! Is she coming to?" her Mother shouted.

"Michelle, just drive and watch the road!" her Father yelled.

Eve sat up and rubbed her blistered forehead with her left hand. Her right hand was swollen. "Why is everyone shouting? What happened?"

"You got your butt handed to you, is what happened! I warned you about them pitty-patty kicks!" Gwen was laughing and crying at the same time.

"Eve! Eve, you're OK? Thank you, Jesus!" her Mother exclaimed.

"I'm good. I'm OK. Outside of feeling like I got hit by a truck, I'm fine."

"What is the last thing you remember?" Ana queried, as she wiped her tears.

218

"Being head-butted."

"We only saw the last few seconds but it seems his head-butt rendered you both unconscious. One of the boys we saw retrieved you," Ana offered.

"And Dave? The antidote?" Eve asked.

"We secured the antidote and Dave got away. The gunman was only able to get off the one shot. He then fell from the roof."

"We secured the antidote. He fell from the roof," Gwen said, mimicking Ana's emotionless speech pattern perfectly. "Please! You really think that dude slipped on a banana peel and fell from the roof?"

"Regardless, I readily administered it to the three of us."

"Why do I even bother?" Gwen exclaimed, throwing her hands in the air in frustration, "Eve, the meeting place was a kill box! Gunman adjacent to the meeting spot. Two gunmen on higher ground."

"Wait… two gunman on higher ground?"

"Yeah! One got thrown off a building, the other jumped from a different building! He almost landed on top of us! Mom took him out with the car!"

"Not intentionally!" their mother shouted, defensively.

"So Mom hit him going full speed, right? And he flew, like, twenty feet! He put a large dent in a small car and just shook it off like it was nothing!"

"So what happened after that?"

"Me and Dad jumped in the car, Mom busted a U-turn, and your gang member boyfriend put you in the car. We then got the heck out of Dodge!"

"Did anyone grab my blouse?"

Chapter 15

It was the last week of school. There had not been any pranks to the school or staff all year. The feeling was that it couldn't last. Anxious teachers were becoming irritable with each other and with their students. They openly discussed who was going to be the next Mr. Freedman. The school petitioned to waive the final fire drill of the year. The petition was denied. The school board did not recognize the threat of Gwendolyn Parker as a legitimate reason to violate state law. The only teacher not concerned about any potential calamities was Mr. Little.

This is absurd! Mr. Little thought, as the fire alarm went off as scheduled. Mr. Little was not pleased with the Parker girls being treated differently than other students. Eve had been absent from school and no explanation would be required if she chose to return. Also, Eve was the only student Mr. Little knew of who could attack a popular student athlete and suffer no repercussions. And although Ana was some type of math savant she was also a definite basket case. The principal told him it was OK if Ana slept in class and he should be thankful that's all she did. And he'd heard about Gwen's exploits before he'd even started working at this school. The school had plans for fires, tornadoes, and Gwen. It was surreal.

Once outside with his students, Mr. Little saw school secretary Tammy Boggs, alongside Mr. Jones, hurrying towards him. Mr. Little shook his head. This school had two security guards and the only thing they guarded was the coffee machine.

Out of breath, Ms. Boggs mumbled, "Have you seen the Target?"

"Excuse me?"

"The Target! We are looking for the Target!" Ms. Boggs repeated, scanning the crowd of students.

"What target are you looking for?"

Ms. Boggs leaned in. "Gwen Parker."

"No, Ms. Boggs. I haven't seen the target."

Ms. Boggs spoke into a walkie-talkie: "I do not have a visual, repeat, I do not have a visual of the Target, over."

"Mrs. Boggs, we need a visual... I repeat, we need a visual. You are the field coordinator for this period, so please locate the target immediately, over," replied a voice that sounded like Dr. Gupta.

"Roger that, over," replied Mrs. Boggs.

"Mr. Little, have you checked the parking lot?"

"No, I haven't. Isn't that the job of, you know... the security guard?" The level of incompetence at this school was ridiculous.

"The union revised their contract when they found out who the Target's grandmother was. Josephine represented the union in a dispute with the city a few years back."

"So, basically, this school has a security guard who's excluded from performing specific security functions! Are you on medication? What is wrong with you people? And all this is because of Gwen Parker?"

"Mr. Little! Please keep your voice down! We were told by legal not to say her name."

"Fine! I'll go! But this is not in my contract!" interjected Mr. Jones, as he headed toward the teacher's parking lot.

"Thank goodness. Thank you, Mr. Jones," exclaimed Ms. Boggs, before she was pre-empted by the walkie-talkie.

"I have a visual, repeat... I have a visual of the target, over," Mrs. Adams announced over the air.

"Thank goodness! Mrs. Adams, bless... Oh my God! What is that? Is that a fire? A bomb?" Ms. Boggs was pointing to a cloud of purple and red smoke billowing from the far side of the school. "Oh my God! She's trying to blow up the school!" Ms. Boggs shouted in complete panic, before fainting in Mr. Little arms.

The majority of staff rushed over to check out the smoke. The principal's voice came over the walkie-talkie asking everyone to stay calm and stay with their students. It was too late.

The students clapped and cheered the smoke. Mr. Little and the few teachers who were left could not control all of them. They began to run around looking for friends from other classes. Pandemonium ensued. It took a while to verify that the smoke was a couple of colored smoke bombs placed in trash dumpsters. It took even more time for the teachers to regroup, calm their students, organize them, perform a headcount, and relocate the "target." Shortly thereafter, a fire truck, police car, and a local news car arrived. During the panic, someone had called the fire department, telling them the school was actually on fire. It being a slow news day, the local news station showed up as well. Needless to say, everyone was a bit miffed about the colossal waste of time... until they found Mr. Little's motorcycle.

***

Gwen was sitting on the living room couch. Barry was looking down at her. He was not pleased.

"Did you duct tape Mr. Little's motorcycle to the roof of the gym?"

"Huh?" said Gwen. Her sisters stood in the hallway watching, and trying not to laugh.

"You heard me. Did. You. Tape. Mr. Little's. Motorcycle. to the roof of the gym?"

"Why would I do that?"

"That is not the question, Gwendolyn. And Mr. Little is furious. He is threatening to sue. And Ms. Boggs fainted."

"Ms. Boggs faints every year. It's, like, in the schedule or something. She fainted last year at a basketball game," Eve explained, from the hallway.

"Eve, please. And don't think I forgot about you beating up that poor kid in gym class." Eve's contusion was gone from her forehead. Ana had also reset Eve's foot and hand and wrapped both in a cast, which Barry had no idea she could do. Ana's IQ, Eve's speed, and Gwen's strength were a constant wonderment to him. His three amazing daughters were now more amazing, but Gwen's antics had to stop. The family had literally and figuratively dodged bullets and the last thing they needed was more attention.

"Why does everyone always blame me for everything? Besides, Mr. Little is a terrible teacher, so anything that might incentivize him to spend less time on his hair and more on his students should be celebrated. I'm just sayin…"

"I know how it was done!" Ana offered.

"Did you see Gwen do it?" Barry said, after closing his mouth from the shock of Gwen's statement.

"No. Of course not. But if someone with prodigious strength could survive a twenty feet drop, and had rope and duct tape, the entire ordeal could be undertaken in approximately 11.3 minutes."

"So, you are saying you know or have proof Gwen did it?" asked Eve.

"Who's talking about Gwen? I said someone."

"Oh, right. Yeah, 'someone' who is super strong but not necessarily Gwen. Got it!"

"Eve, you are making assumptions. I am simply inferring that taping a motorcycle to the roof of the gym is not insurmountable. I never said Gwen's name."

"So this someone would have to be as strong as Gwen, be mischievous like Gwen, but all this is completely coincidental, right? I mean it could be anybody, right?" Eve laughed.

"Gwen, this is serious. This has to stop! You are too old for this type of behavior! We are all still incredibly embarrassed about what happened to poor Mr. Freedman last year—"

"Why am I getting blamed for a hundred-year-old teacher who can't control his bowel movements? Maybe he had too much fiber in his diet!" Gwen shouted, as she crossed her arms and stuck out her lip. Ana and Eve doubled over in laughter.

"That isn't funny! And Gwen, you know he couldn't make it to the bathroom because someone put something in his coffee."

"I keep telling everyone that I never put anything in his coffee. Honest! But no one ever believes me!"

"It would be less risky to put it in his cup," Ana offered.

"Shut up, Ana! Before I tell Dad you were selling candy again. Oops!" Gwen feigned astonishment while covering her mouth.

"Is that true, Ana?"

"So does this mean I still can't have a house like Ana?" interrupted Gwen.

"Gwen, I never said that! I never promised you a house! And you're still in trouble!"

"OK, then let me have some drums and we can call it even."

"No, Gwen! No drums and no house! And stop changing the subject!"

"But you promised!"

"Gwen, go to your room! Now!" Barry was frustrated. He had no idea how he and Michelle were going to manage the girls with their special abilities. The antidote they'd assumed would relieve them of their powers had done no such thing. The antidote relieved them of the headaches and nosebleeds that were a direct result of their powers. Headaches and nosebleeds he and Michelle had known nothing about. But at least Dave had left a message saying the external threat had been neutralized, although precautions were still needed. However, precautions and the Parker girls did not go hand-in-hand. *Summer can't get here soon enough!* Barry thought.

Chapter 16

"No! Your defender has to commit first! You can't crossover until I commit to blocking your path to the basket. Try it again!" Eve yelled at Gwen. They were in their driveway on a bright, sunny Saturday morning. It was the last Saturday of June and the day of the Parker family's annual picnic. Eve and her sisters had been going at it all morning. Eve, now fully healed, had resumed basketball, working out, and sparring three weeks ago.

"Stop shouting at me!" Gwen shouted.

"I'm not shouting!" Eve shouted back. "And you have to sell it! Make your defender commit, then crossover. If I don't commit, drive to the basket. Now do it again! They'll be here any minute." Basketball was a great distraction for Eve. It allowed her to have fun. To be carefree and unafraid. She had been experiencing nightmares on nights she was lucky enough to fall asleep; every time she closed her eyes she saw a big knife coming at her. Those visions haunted Eve. They drove her to push herself past exhaustion when working out. She kept thinking that if she only worked hard enough she'd be too tired to have nightmares. She was wrong.

"Stop swiping at the ball!" Gwen shouted.

"It's called defense! Now drive... There you go! Good! Again!" Basketball was a great distraction. But a distraction is all it was. All Eve wanted to do now was spar, fight; she had to get faster, stronger. Eve was better at fighting than she was at anything, and Eve was good at a lot of things. But being good at something had never been enough for her—she had to be the best.

"I did it! I did it!" Gwen shouted, after successfully crossing Eve over and driving to the basket for a layup.

"Again! Get the ball and do it again. And don't get too excited. We still need to work on your spin move!" Basketball was a great distraction—it occupied Eve's mind; it provided normalcy, and she needed that. Because when it was still, when it was quiet, Eve could not control her thoughts. She mostly thought of herself during those still, quiet times, and those thoughts were troubling. This had been a year of self-discovery and yet Eve still didn't quite know who she was. She knew she could be brave and face death without flinching, but she also knew she suffered no moral qualms about hurting innocent people to achieve her goals. Eve didn't know what that said about her and those thoughts haunted her as much as the knife.

"They're here," Ana said, as a late model SUV turned the corner and pulled into their driveway. As usual, Ana had her hair in afro puffs. Her purple umbrella shaded her while she sipped lemonade. She had been providing commentary and instructions to both Eve and Gwen until Gwen threatened to throw her out a window.

"Gwenny!" Walter jumped out the car.

Emmitt came from around the car, snatched the basketball from Gwen, took two dribbles toward the basket, and did a 360-degree dunk effortlessly. Grabbing the ball on the bounce, he tossed it back to Gwen, saying, "That's how you do it, cousin!"

"Boy, if you don't start getting the stuff out the back!" his mother boomed. Aunt Alicia was a light-skinned, wide-bodied woman who stood six feet two. She was a math teacher and girl's high school basketball coach at the same school her two sons and nephew attended. She did not suffer fools gladly. Both her sons dutifully obeyed.

"You girls better come here and give me a kiss!" she bellowed. It was not a request.

Uncle Baldwin pulled up a minute later in his SUV. It was the exact same type as Benjamin's, except his was white while Benjamin's was black. He hopped out first, followed by his two children, Antoinette—a college sophomore—and Antonio. His wife Alondra, a petite, curvy Colombian woman, was the last one out. She threw her long, single-braided hair over her shoulder, while her large almond eyes sparkled at the sight of the girls. Her wide smile displayed prominent cheekbones. Eve thought if there was a more beautiful woman sans makeup, she hadn't met her.

"Cousins!" Antoinette yelled, giving all the girls hugs. Antoinette was just as beautiful as her mother, but was tall and statuesque. Antonio patiently waited his turn and it was easy to see why he caused hearts to flutter wherever he went. He had his father's strong, athletic build complemented by his mother's skin tone and features.

"All right, girls! Bring it in. Time to get cleaned up!" Michelle motioned everyone inside from the front door.

"Aww, Mom! One more game!" Gwen protested.

"Young lady, get your butt in this house and get in some water!"

Eve was enjoying herself with her family two hours later. She was sitting at the picnic table with her sisters and cousins. The adults were relaxing in the gazebo further back. The food was delicious, but it was the camaraderie and fellowship that provided Eve the nourishment she craved. She heard the front door bell and a minute later, Kang, Amy, Elizabeth, and Tyler walked out on the deck. Tyler looked around and their eyes met; Eve turned away while she tapped Antoinette on the shoulder and they both slipped away.

***

Tyler was amazed at the Parkers' house. It was almost as big as Toni's, though not as opulent. The grass looked like it was cut with scissors, there were colorful flowers and bushes all along the privacy fence, and the gazebo was bigger than his family's apartment.

Gwen came to meet them. "Hey, guys. What's up?" Gwen couldn't shake hands because one held a plate full of ribs, the other was painted with barbecue sauce.

Tyler smiled at Gwen as she went to work on the ribs. "Hey, Gwen, phat crib… and who owns the 1967 all-white convertible Eldorado with the whitewalls?"

"Gwen, is your grandmother here? I need to thank her," Elizabeth interjected.

Ana, who was now standing next to Gwen, said, "Sure… she is right over there, come on."

Tyler looked around. "Wait! Wait! Josephine Jefferson is really here? Really?"

"First, that's my grandfather's Cadillac. He only drives the older model cars that he works on himself. And yeah, my grams is here, but she prefers Mrs. Harris in private settings." Gwen motioned toward the gazebo.

"Wow! And your cousins are here too! Those cats is off the chain! Walter has broken every running back record in the state. Antonio has to be the best point guard and quarterback in the city, and don't get me started on Emmitt; you can't turn on the news without seeing him dunking on somebody."

"Yeah, they're awesome," Gwen offered, grinning from ear to ear.

"True dat. But I heard their fathers and uncles was just as nice back in the day. That would be your pops, right?"

"Uh, no! Our dad is more of a mathlete!" Gwen laughed hysterically at her own joke. The laughter caused a rib to fall from her plate. "Freeze!" she yelled, holding her arm protectively over the rib. "Nobody moves and nobody gets hurt!" Everyone froze. Gwen carefully picked up the rib, kissed it, and held it above her head like Excalibur, before eating it like nothing had happened.

"So then, he owns a rap label?" continued Tyler.

"Please! Have you met my dad? Does he strike you as the rap mogul type?" laughed Gwen.

"Seriously, the Parker boys have an uncle who owns a rap label. A couple of my boyz signed with him. For a few hundred dollars he's going to help them cut a demo."

"Owns a rap label? Classic! I have to call Uncle Brian," laughed Gwen.

Ana smiled, shaking her head. "Come on Elizabeth, my grandmother is over here. Tyler, I strongly advise you to pull up your pants. Trust me on this."

"I told him!" Kang laughed, as they followed Ana and Gwen.

"Grams, this is Elizabeth. Her mother is Mrs. Newman. She wanted to say hello," Ana announced.

Tyler could tell Elizabeth was nervous. They all were.

"Hello, Mrs. Jefferson, I mean Mrs. Harris. I, I, just wanted to thank you for all the help you gave my mom."

"Baby, don't worry about thanking me yet. I didn't help Holly. I invested in Holly and I expect a return on my investment. Holly is a very bright and ambitious woman with a lot of personality. I mean, a lot of personality. I have high expectations for her so don't be thanking me just yet. And how have you been?"

"I'm, I've been OK."

"Well, Gwen tells me you are quite the pianist and basketball player? And I hope you have homeowners insurance. You are going to need it if you are hanging around that child. That girl know she a mess!" Josephine laughed wholeheartedly.

Tyler was still starstruck but didn't think Elizabeth's circumstances warranted all the attention she received. She still lived in a phat house paid for by a father she refused to talk to. And her mother was now working at the most prestigious law firm in the country. And one of the most powerful women in America was paying for her to finish law school. *Rich people don't fall down, they fall up,* Tyler thought.

"Hey Kang, how have you been, baby? And how is your sister?"

While Josephine addressed Kang, Tyler took in every detail of her. Her tone was conversational and lighthearted, unlike the precise academic tone she used in press conferences. She looked shorter and thinner than on TV. Her face was thin like Ana's, and her short silver crown of hair gave her a distinguished look. Her attire of linen pants and matching shirt made her look like any other grandmother. And she was smiling. Tyler had seen her over a hundred times on TV and she never smiled.

"I've been good. And my sister is fine. She is home from medical school and helping out at one of my parents' schools. I'm sorry, these are my friends, Tyler and Amy."

"Amy child, you are fierce on that court! I really had high hopes for the team this year. But I must say, hon, it's nice to finally meet you. And you are even more beautiful up close."

"Thanks. Thank you."

"Hey, babe, this is Amy. She plays ball with the girls." Josephine turned to an older gentleman reading a paper.

Without looking up from his paper, the older gentleman replied, "I know who Amy is. The girl is a good rebounder and has a nice ten foot jumper."

"Y'all have to excuse my husband." Mrs. Jefferson laughed.

Tyler carefully observed the husband of Mrs. Josephine Jefferson-Harris. He was thin and of medium height. His neatly trimmed

233

silver afro was matched by a small silver mustache that stood out against his dark, weathered face.

"So you the Tyler Eve likes. My, you are cute."

Mr. Harris peered at Tyler over his reading glasses. "Eve is too young to be liking anybody." His silver mustache and afro reflected the light. His eyes were almost as dark as his skin. "Well, Tyler, what are your intentions with my grandbaby?"

Tyler smiled then closed his mouth. He checked to see if anyone else was smiling. He couldn't tell if Mr. Harris was joking. *I thought barbecues are supposed to be fun,* Tyler thought.

Josephine threw her head back laughing, and hit her husband on the arm. "Oh, Larry, stop it! Leave the boy alone and be nice for once."

"I am nice. I'm always nice… so Tyler, where you from?" Lawrence's gruff tone didn't change but his face softened a bit.

Put at ease by Josephine's infectious laugh, Tyler recited his address.

"That's my old neighborhood. I run an auto shop there. But it's a pretty rough area and a long way from the suburbs. What you doing way out here?"

"Larry, will you please leave the boy alone and let him enjoy himself! Thank you, Tyler. You and your friends better go get some food before Ana and Gwen eat everything. Lord knows where they put it all. They ain't big as a minute!"

Gwen led the party back to the deck where the food table was set up, and everyone helped themselves. They then followed her over to a picnic table that was shielded from the sun by a large canopy.

"Let me finish! Like I was saying… that is the game I would have scored fifty points if coach hadn't pulled me!" Emmitt was telling anyone who would listen.

"Naw, dawg… I heard you the first ten times. I just have a problem with your math! You had twenty-nine points by the end of the third quarter! So you telling us you would have scored twenty-one points in the fourth? Pleeeease! You killin me!" mocked Antonio.

"Give it a rest… hey, Kang, I got your messages but I've been busy." Walter's voice was so deep it caught Tyler by surprise.

Walter was sitting next to Gwen and Ana on one side of the picnic table, facing Antonio and Emmitt on the other side.

"I've been working out with the high school team, so it's cool," Kang replied.

"Hey, Kang, we can't help you this year anyway, because you the enemy now. And if your team makes the playoffs we going to have to put a hurtin' on ya!" taunted Emmitt, while smashing his fist into his open palm.

"What are you talking about? You never work out with us anyway!" Antonio replied.

"I thought I told you two knuckleheads to give it a rest? I was talking to Kang… So Kang, what your bench and squat look like now?" Emmitt and Antonio went silent under Walter's glare.

"I got my bench up to two-forty-five, and I'm squatting three plates."

"Nice. Pretty boy quarterbacks don't usually lift like that. Keep up the hard work. I'm going to email you the workout my college

235

coaches have us doing," Walter replied as he got up to get seconds, followed by the rest of the table.

Tyler was on his second plate when Eve reappeared. Gone were the T-shirt and shorts she had previously worn. She was now wearing a short, white summer dress. Her natural had a large part on the side with a red flower in it. Her lip gloss drew attention to her pearly white teeth, full lips, and nervous smile.

Tyler stared. His heart skipped a beat. She was all he thought about. Elizabeth and Amy both got up to go greet Eve.

"Hey, Tyler, right? Come down here for a minute and let me holla at ya." Walter's tone indicated refusing him was not an option. The table went silent. Tyler looked at Kang opposite him for support; Kang coughed and started studying the corn on his plate like it was algebra. Tyler slowly got up, swearing under his breath. He couldn't remember having had a worse time at a barbecue.

Walter motioned for Antonio and Emmitt to slide down so Tyler could sit facing him. As Tyler took a seat, Walter purposely looked him up and down. "So, you the cat that broke my little cousin's heart, right?" Tyler looked Walter in the eye and tried to ignore his massive arms. Tyler didn't consider himself a punk. In his neighborhood he had a well-deserved reputation for being nice with his hands. But everyone knew you didn't mess with the Parker boys.

Tyler acted as cool as he could while rubbing the back of his neck. "We just friends."

"Just friends, huh? I'm only going to tell you this once, playa… them three girls are my heart. I'll do anything for them. When I found out my little cousin had her nose wide open for some cat from the city I asked around about you... What do you think I found out?"

Tyler didn't respond to Walter's question. He thought he was never going to another barbecue as long as he lived.

Walter continued. "I found out you a pretty cool cat. Got your head on straight, got some decent skills on the football field and basketball court. No one I talked to had anything bad to say about you."

"Leave him alone, Walt. He straight," Antonio offered.

"Oh, I know he straight... My man, what I'm trying to relay to you is this... I would hate to lose my scholarship for putting in work on some knucklehead that can't keep his hands to himself. Ya feel me?"

"Boy, please! Ain't nobody scared of you!" Antoinette walked up and announced her presence with an exclamation point. "Hi, Tyler, I'm Antoinette... Eve's cousin." She extended her right hand and slapped Walter in the back of his head with her left. Tyler cautiously shook her hand. She had a firm grip, confident demeanor, and commanding presence. He didn't know if he should be more scared of her or Walter.

"Girl, how many times do I have to tell you to keep your hands to yourself? Don't you have some Shakespeare to read or something?" Walter smiled, rubbing the back of his head to laughter from the table.

"That's as bad as the whooping me and Ana put on you last year on the court!" Emmitt laughed.

"Now there you go! You know me and Eve went undefeated last year! And if I remember right she crossed you up more than a few times!" Antonio said.

"You killin' me, dawg! Outside of me, Ana has the best jump shot in the family! That girl is silky smooth and I taught her everything she knows!"

"Well, why don't you teach the girl some defense? Oh, my bad… that's something you know nothing about!"

"And everyone knows defense and rebounding wins championships! Ain't that right, Gwenny?" Walter interjected, as Gwen smiled in agreement.

"There's a difference between mugging someone and playing defense. As many games as you been kicked out this year you should know that by now. Besides, you and Gwen didn't win a game last year!" taunted Emmitt.

"We can go again! I got the ball in the car!" Antonio shouted, jumping up.

"Antonio, sit your butt down! Who wants to play basketball as hot as it is?" interjected Antoinette. "Besides, Eve is looking too cute right now. She has too much charisma to be wasting it on the court, anyway. That girl needs to be up on the stage!"

"Girl, you need to go somewhere with that! You've been trying to convert her to the dark side for years! How she gonna work on her crossover in drama class!" Antonio laughed.

Tyler walked over to Eve. "Hey, Eve."

"Hey, Tyler. What are you doing here?"

"Kang's sister's in town. She stopped by at your parents' house last week to say hi. You guys were at your grandmother's or something, but your mother invited us. I thought you knew we were coming?"

"Somehow that slipped my parents' mind." Eve laughed.

"Right, right. So, um, Eve. I want to say, I would like to say that I am sorry. You know, about everything." Eve was so stunning everything around her was dull by comparison. She was the absolute most beautiful and amazing person he had ever met and he'd blown a gasket because she wanted him to meet her parents.

"No, Tyler, I'm sorry. I was wrong. I was selfish. I—"

"Eve, stop. You wanted me to meet your parents. That's not something that needs an apology." Everyone was watching, but Tyler did not care. Tyler didn't know if it was destiny, or chance that had led to this exact moment, but he knew it might not last. Eve was American royalty. Her great-grandfather was a Tuskegee airman and war hero. Her grandmother was one of the most respected women in America, if not the world. Tyler was a cliché. There was a kid like him in every inner city in America. Poor, one-parent home, no relationship with his father. His story was so common even his tragedies didn't warrant special attention. When his brother was killed it was just another gang member dead. The narrative being more important than facts, him not being in a gang was irrelevant. The only thing special about Tyler were his friends... and Eve. And he was going to hold on to that as long as he could.

Eve grabbed his hand, leading him back to the picnic table. He felt lightheaded. They sat across from each other. "So, Eve, how have you been? You missed the last month of school and Amy said something about you seeing a specialist?"

"I'm OK, Tyler, really. I'm OK now."

"Well, it's just that, you know, everyone says you fainted and was bleeding. And I never said anything, but… every time I touched you, you felt really warm. Like a fever or something."

"You trying to tell me I'm hot?" Eve laughed. "Don't worry. I was sick. I got better."

Tyler cleared his throat, "'When peoples care for you and cry for you, they can straighten out your soul.'"

"That was beautiful. I knew you would like Langston Hughes. Now look at you, trying to get all deep."

"Baby, I got layers." They both laughed. When they stopped, Tyler softly grabbed her hand. He couldn't stop looking at her. Her dark skin contrasted against her white dress, the flower in her hair, her smile; she was entrancing. *This is the best barbecue ever!* Tyler thought.

Three hours later, the barbecue was winding down. Benjamin and Baldwin and their families started loading up. Josephine and Lawrence offered a ride home to Tyler; Lawrence indicated it was not up for debate. Kang's sister picked up Kang, Amy, and Elizabeth. Eve and Tyler watched them leave from the driveway. Tyler wanted to kiss Eve on the lips, but with Walter and everyone watching he settled for her cheek. He said his goodbyes and hopped in the back of the '67 El-dog with whitewalls. He couldn't believe it—Josephine Jefferson and her husband, Mr. Lawrence Harris, were going to personally drive him home. Maybe he wasn't a cliché after all.

***

Eve watched Tyler leave with her grandparents. Surrounded by family she felt beautiful. She felt loved. She felt special.

"Alright, baby bruh." Benjamin embraced Barry in a bear hug. "We better hit that road."

"Okay, Benj. Don't let them work you too hard at the post office, man."

"I'll be OK, baby bruh. Let's hit it, boys."

"I'm right behind you, Benj," Baldwin said. "Later, baby bruh."

The house was quiet, serene. The year had been so hectic the Parker family barely had time to breathe. They commenced to cleaning up the kitchen and picnic area. They worked quietly while listening to music. All the cleaning was completed within an hour.

Michelle winked at Barry. "Babe, care to join me for a glass of wine? Upstairs?"

"Ahem. Sure, let me take out the trash. I'll be right up!"

After their father went upstairs, the girls sat at the breakfast bar in silence. Marvin Gaye drifted down from their parents' room. It had been a while since her parents had played Marvin. Over a year. Eve appreciated the stillness. She thought about everything that had happened over the school year. A smile crossed her face. She now knew they were not freaks. She knew that more than anything. But they were not heroes either; at least not yet.

Made in the USA
Charleston, SC
28 March 2014